TO HER SURPRISE, THE DOOR OPENED AS NICKY TUGGED AT IT.

"I don't believe it!" Adam exclaimed. Then he ran for the door, with Kendra right behind him. Josh and Nathan stayed where they were.

There was a jungle outside the back door, and bright sunlight. It wasn't the same jungle that they had seen from the front window, though. This looked a lot more alien. Instead of trees, there were huge ferns. There were no flowers, but there were odd growths that Kendra couldn't identify. Tall grasses were all over the place, and small pools of mud. It had obviously finished raining quite recently, wherever this was.

As Kendra stared out, she saw something moving in the jungle. She gasped as a huge insect buzzed between the trees. She'd caught a glimpse of something that was a shimmering blue color, and at least a foot from wing to wing. There were no such insects. It looked like a dragonfly, but it was way too big for one. Nothing like that had lived since . . .

Since the days of the dinosaurs . . .

"Oh my God," she whispered.

D0967426

ARE YOU AFRAID OF THE DARK?™ novels

Available from MINSTREL Books

NICKELODEON®

Are You Afraid of the Dark?™

THE TALE OF THE
RESTLESS HOUSE

JOHN PEEL

A
MINSTREL®
BOOK

PUBLISHED BY POCKET BOOKS

New York   London   Toronto   Sydney   Tokyo   Singapore

A MINSTREL PAPERBACK *Original*

 A Minstrel Book published by
POCKET BOOKS, a division of Simon & Schuster Inc.
1230 Avenue of the Americas, New York, NY 10020

© 1995 Viacom International Inc. All rights reserved. Based on the Nickelodeon series entitled "Are You Afraid of the Dark?" © 1992–1994 CINAR. All rights reserved.

ISBN: 0-671-52547-6

First Minstrel Books printing July 1995

10 9 8 7 6 5 4

A MINSTREL BOOK and colophon are registered trademarks of Simon & Schuster Inc.

NICKELODEON and all related titles, logos, and characters are trademarks of Viacom International Inc.

Cover photography by Barbara Nitke and Jonathan Wenk

Printed in the U.S.A.

This one is for Michael and Helen Peel.

THE KEY IS AFRAID OF THE DARK

PROLOGUE

Are you afraid of the dark?

We all are sometimes, aren't we? Sometimes without reason and sometimes there's a very good reason indeed to be afraid. Very *afraid.*

Welcome to the latest meeting of the Midnight Society. My name is Samantha, but I prefer to be called Sam. You're more than welcome to join us, as I have a special story to tell. You've all heard stories about haunted houses, I'm sure . . . but nothing like the house in this *story. It's definitely a spooky place, but it isn't haunted—at least, not in the usual way.*

But in a very unusual *way . . .*

The heroine of this story is a young girl called Kendra. She doesn't start out that way, though. In fact, when the story begins, Kendra's made a cou-

ple of very bad mistakes. First of all, she's made some pretty questionable friends. Secondly, she's let them talk her into doing something she should never have agreed to. She's agreed to spend the night in that haunted house I just mentioned. What she doesn't yet know is that you can get into the house very easily.

Getting out, on the other hand, may be impossible.

Submitted for the approval of the Midnight Society, I call this story . . .

The Tale of the Restless House.

CHAPTER 1

Ever since Kendra Collins had been little, the old Hawkins House had scared her. It was several blocks from her home, but on the way she took to school each day. The house didn't *look* evil, but there was almost a stench of horror about the place. It was a two-story house, with a large front porch perfect for a swing or a rocking chair. Except that nobody lived at the Hawkins House anymore, so there was never anything on the porch other than the leaves in the fall and the snow in winter.

There was a once-white picket fence around the house, which kept the untidy garden in check. Nobody ever seemed to cut the lawn, yet it was still fairly neat. And there were lots of lilacs and fire bushes that bloomed at the right season, giving the place a splash of color from time to time. Somebody must have owned the house, but nobody lived there. And, strangely, nobody seemed to want to sell the house, either. Plenty of people might have been interested in buying such a pleasant-looking house. If they didn't know better.

It didn't *look* haunted. At least, not in the daytime.

But at night ... Well, Kendra tried to avoid going anywhere near the place at night. If you went past it some nights, noises could be heard inside. Strange noises, more like roaring than screaming, and more like screaming than talking. Lights would flicker on and off in some of the rooms. And more than once passersby had seen people inside the house.

Those of Kendra's friends who were skeptical claimed it was just kids playing, or maybe homeless people who stayed a night or so in the abandoned house and then moved on. But Kendra didn't believe that. She'd heard plenty of stories about people passing by the Hawkins House, but never of anyone who'd ever set foot inside it. At least, nobody who was ever seen again.

Until now.

She stared blankly at Nathan Forrester, thinking that she must have misheard him. "What?" she asked.

"Jeez, pay attention, will you?" Nathan growled, rolling his eyes. He glared down at

4

Kendra. "I said that this is going to be the best prank we've ever pulled on anyone." He gestured over his shoulder at the Hawkins House. Since it was daytime, the place looked cheerfully innocent. "In there."

"In that place?" Kendra felt slightly sick. "You want us to go in *there?*"

"Come on, Kennie," begged Nicole Manners. "Don't wimp out on us now, huh?"

Kendra glanced over at her best friend. Nicole was wearing her *Kendra, you're embarrassing me* expression again. She was clutching her boyfriend, Joshua Drake, as if afraid he'd wander away if left unattended. Sometimes Kendra wondered why she was friends with Nicole at all if Nicky found her that embarrassing. They really weren't much alike: Kendra had long, dark brown hair that hung down to the small of her back. Nicole had a frizzy head of tight blond curls. Their personalities matched just about as well as their hair. Yet Kendra and Nicky had been together almost forever, aside from a few times when they'd gotten mad at one another. Kendra had always given in at the end and made up. They lived next door to one another and had grown up together. At least, Kendra thought, *she'd* grown up. She had her doubts about Nicky.

"Don't tell us you're *scared?*" sneered Nathan, "of the 'haunted house'?"

5

Josh smirked. "You don't believe in ghosts, do you?"

"No," said Kendra, as firmly as she could. "Of course not." She wasn't sure whether she was lying or not. "It's just that . . ."

"It's just what?" demanded Nathan. "Are you with us or not?"

Kendra didn't want to make a decision. She didn't exactly believe that the Hawkins House was haunted. On the other hand, there was certainly something very odd and scary about it. Still, if she backed down now, she knew that Nathan and Josh would certainly use her refusal to make fun of her. That was the sort of kids they were. And she didn't need to think twice about what Nicky would say. "I guess I am," she finally said miserably. "I just don't like it too much."

"Ah, that's okay," Nathan said, his humor restored. "You don't have to do much. I'll do all the work." He lifted his backpack. "I've got everything we need in here to make the place look like it's *really* haunted. I'll go in now and set it up."

That part at least pleased Kendra. She could get out of going in there right now. Maybe she could work up her courage before she had to venture inside. "So what do I have to do?" she asked.

Nathan grinned wickedly. "Call up Adam Ingram," he said. "Invite him over to double with

6

you, Nicole, and Josh. Then bring him here at sunset."

"Adam Ingram?" Kendra asked, frowning. He was a semi–cute-looking guy in their class, but not one she'd paid much attention to. He was a little too serious, and really into computers and stuff. He'd always struck her as a nerd in the making. "Why him?"

"Jeez." Nathan rolled his eyes again. "One," he said, counting on his fingers, "the guy's the biggest wuss in school. He'll probably keel over in a faint when he sees what I've got lined up. He really does believe in ghosts. And two, he's got the hots for you."

Kendra found herself blushing. "He *what?*"

"Come on, Kennie," said Nicky with a sigh. "Haven't you noticed all those looks he's been giving you?"

"Yeah," agreed Josh. "He practically has to carry a bucket when you're around to catch all his drool in."

Wishing she wasn't so obviously red-faced, Kendra muttered, "You've got to be kidding." She'd never noticed any interest from Adam. Then again, she hardly ever noticed Adam at all. Her friends might well be right, and she just hadn't seen it.

Mistaking what she meant, Nathan obviously thought she simply didn't like the idea of going with Adam. "Come on," he pleaded. "It won't be a *real* date. I'm not asking you to trade spit with him or anything. Just pretend you like him to get him here."

Kendra bit her lip uncertainly. She didn't know what to say. If she didn't go along with her friends' plans, they'd be really mad at her. On the other hand, it didn't feel right to sucker Adam the way they wanted her to. Okay, she didn't care for him or anything, but if he did have a crush on her, it would be pretty horrible to use it for a joke. But "pretty horrible" would describe Nicky's reaction if she backed out.

"Maybe that's not it," Nicky said, grinning shyly. "Maybe *she's* got the hots for him, too. And she doesn't want him to look like a jerk in case he won't go out with her for real."

"That's not true," Kendra answered, blushing again. "I don't care about Adam Ingram one way or the other."

"So what's the problem then?" demanded Nathan. "Are you going to do this? Or are you going to wimp out on us and let us down?"

Kendra wanted to avoid the whole thing, but she simply couldn't think of a good excuse. She knew what would happen if she refused. But what about if she agreed? What would it do to Adam? What would he think of her then? Still, what did she care *what* he thought of her? His opinion didn't mean anything to her. It wasn't her fault that Adam had a crush on her. Now that she

8

knew about it, she knew she'd never be able to see him in class again without realizing he was staring at her. Maybe it was best if she made it plain to him that she didn't want him drooling over her.

"All right," she finally said. "I'll give him a call." Hope flared inside her. "But he probably won't be able to make it tonight anyway."

"Sure he will," Nicky informed her. "I already asked him if he could." She handed over a scrap of paper. "That's his phone number. I told him you'd call to arrange things."

Kendra felt angry. "You already did it without even asking me?" she growled.

"Well, we just asked you," Nathan snapped back. "And you said yes, so stop complaining. We didn't want to run the chance he wouldn't be able to make it, okay? So get going and give him a call."

"And try and sound like you *mean* it," suggested Nicky. "Be enthusiastic and happy. Like it'll be *fun.*"

Josh grinned. " 'Cause it will be," he added. "But not for Adam!"

Kendra felt as if she'd been manipulated. But she *had* agreed to go through with it, and she couldn't back out now. It didn't seem right, but there was nothing she could do about that now. Besides, what harm could there really be in scaring a wuss like Adam Ingram? With a sigh, she

9

slipped his phone number into her bag and started off for home.

"See you at six!" Nicky called. "We'll be over to get you!" She clung to Joshua, and they headed off their own way.

Whistling happily to himself, Nathan shouldered his backpack and vaulted the fence into the yard of the Hawkins House. This was going to be one evening none of them would forget for a long time. Especially that jerk Ingram! He bounded up onto the porch and crossed to the front door. He turned the handle, and the door opened easily. Grinning, Nathan entered and then closed the door behind him.

It was unfortunate that Kendra, Nicole, and Joshua were too far away from the house by now. It meant that none of them heard Nathan's screams. None of them knew until later that they'd just agreed to the biggest mistake of their lives. . . .

CHAPTER 2

Wishing she could think of some way to back out of everything without getting burned, Kendra slowly dialed Adam's number. She wanted very badly for him not to be home, but he picked up the phone on the second ring. "Uh, hi," she said, flustered and more than a little guilty. "This is Kendra Collins."

"I know," she heard Adam say eagerly. He sounded both excited and scared, and Kendra felt another twinge of guilt. *He really does have a crush on me,* she realized. What Nathan, Nicky, and Josh wanted her to do to Adam was wrong. But she didn't have any choice now. She'd promised to go through with it.

"Uh, Nicky said you'd be up for doubling on a date with her and Josh tonight," she managed to say.

"Are you kidding?" he asked. "In a second. I'd do almost *anything* for a date with you, Kendra."

She found herself blushing, and was annoyed at her reaction. So he was sincere—was that *her* fault? She'd never asked him to have a crush on her. Why should she care about hurting his feelings? He had no right to expect her to like him back, just because he thought she was attractive. "Great," she said, trying to sound as sincere as him. "Why don't you pick me up at six?" she suggested. "I live at—"

"I know where you live," he interrupted. "Nicky told me already."

"Fine," she said, hiding her annoyance. "See you then."

"You bet!"

Since he didn't seem to be at all anxious to hang up, Kendra did. Then she punched one of the cushions on the sofa, wishing it was Adam's face. "What nerve!" she muttered. She knew underneath her anger, though, that she was simply trying to work up the courage to go through with what Nathan had planned. Being angry at Adam would help, even if it wasn't his fault.

But there was no chickening out now. She'd agreed to Nathan's plan, and that was all there was to it. By the end of the evening, they'd all be laughing at Adam Ingram. And he'd certainly drop this stupid crush he had on her!

*   *   *

Adam was, of course, early. He arrived at a quarter to six, very red-faced and wide-eyed. He'd brought her a small bunch of flowers, which irritated Kendra even more. She loved flowers and was determined not to let this gift undermine her intentions. Still, it didn't hurt to appear genuinely pleased to get them. It would make him even less suspicious that anything was going to happen later.

Kendra put the flowers in water, and then took them to her room. Adam followed her, nervous and unsure of himself. He stood in the doorway and glanced around. "Nice room," he said.

"You think so?" Kendra looked around it critically. "I think it's kind of childish, but my folks won't let me update it." She really hated the cutesy pink comforter on her bed, and the light pink paint on the walls.

"I think it looks fine," he disagreed. "Like you—fresh and pretty."

Jeez! Kendra winced. *Talk about corny compliments!* But she could see that he was sincere, and blushed despite herself. "Well, maybe," she said, placing the flowers on her vanity. They did look kind of neat.

Thankfully, she was saved by the doorbell from thinking of anything else to say. "That'll be Nicky and Josh," she said. "You ready to go?"

"Sure." He followed her to the door, where her friends were waiting.

13

"Whoa," said Nicky, grinning. "You guys been getting to know one another better?"

"Just saying hello," Kendra answered, grabbing her coat. It was late fall, and getting cool outside, so she'd need it. It was also getting close to sunset. She called out a good-bye to her mother, who was in the kitchen, and received back the usual instruction not to be home late. Then the four of them headed off together.

Kendra noticed that Adam didn't seem to know what to do with himself. Nicky was wrapped around Josh's arm, as usual, and leading the way. Kendra wasn't too sure what Adam was thinking, but he probably was wishing for some inspiration about what to do or say. Well, a little bit of reassuring him probably wouldn't hurt. She held out her right hand. He looked at it, blushing slightly, so she grabbed his left hand and jerked him toward her gently. "Don't you want to walk with me?" she asked.

His face got redder even in the fading light. "Definitely!" he insisted, interlocking his fingers with hers. "I just didn't want to seem too ... forward."

"Well, relax," Kendra answered. "Holding hands isn't going to get either of us into trouble, okay?" Actually, that wasn't strictly true—it was going to get *him* into a lot of trouble. He just didn't know it yet.

He nodded, looking happy and uncomfortable

at the same time. "So, uh, where are we going?" he asked.

"You'll find out in a little while," Josh said, grinning. "We thought we'd go somewhere where you and Kendra could get to know one another better."

"Yeah," agreed Nicky, matching his grin. "This is, like your first date, isn't it?"

And last, thought Kendra fiercely.

"Uh, yeah," agreed Adam, blushing again.

"We'll soon be there," Josh offered, winking at Kendra.

She wished she could call the whole thing off, but it was too late for that. As they drew closer to the Hawkins House, her skin was starting to get very cold. It had nothing to do with the night, which was actually a bit warmer than she'd expected. It was simply the knowledge of where they were heading. *Get a grip!* she ordered herself. *Those stories are just that—stories! It's not really haunted. Not really.* Then another part of her mind answered: *Liar!*

And then they were there. In the growing gloom, the house didn't look anywhere near as nice or friendly as during the day. The windows started to seem like eyes, and the porch was filling with shadows. Kendra felt a shiver in the base of her spine.

"The Hawkins House?" asked Adam, suddenly

realizing where they were. "You guys want to hang out here?"

"Not *out*," Josh corrected him. "*In.*"

"Inside that place?" The color drained from Adam's face. "Are you crazy?"

"No," answered Nicole. "Are you *chicken?*"

"No," Adam replied. "But I'm not stupid, either. I don't go looking for trouble. And that house is bad news."

"You *are* scared," Josh sneered. "Jeez, I knew it." He rolled his eyes. "You really think there are ghosts in there ready to jump out and frighten you out of your chicken skin?"

Adam shrugged. "It doesn't matter what I think is in there. I'd have to be stupid to go along with this."

Nicky elbowed Kendra far from gently in the ribs. "Are you going to let him run out on you now?" she asked pointedly.

No, I'll be running with him, Kendra thought. But she was well aware of the warning look in her friend's eyes. If she tried to back out now, her life wouldn't be worth living. "Come on, Adam," she said, trying to sound as eager as she could. "It'll be fun in there. We can watch out for one another."

"Yeah," Josh agreed, smiling. "And if you're lucky, Kennie will get scared and need holding *real* tight. Right?"

Adam was wavering. He chewed his lip, nervously glancing at the shadowy house. "It's a pretty dumb idea," he insisted, but without his earlier conviction.

Kendra caught the glance Nicky shot at her: *Do it!* She swallowed her own fears and said, "Come on, Adam. I promise, you can comfort me once we're in there. Okay?"

"Well . . ." But Adam was lost. Kendra could see that. There was no way he was going to back out of this now and look like a chicken in front of her. "I still think it's dumb. But—okay."

"Atta guy," said Nicky, blowing him a kiss. "You won't regret it."

Yes he will, thought Kendra. But she was committed to making him look like a jerk now, despite her feelings. He really was kind of sweet and not so bad looking, either. But she had to go through with this.

Josh led the way. He opened the gate one-handed—Nicky was still firmly attached to his other—and they all went in. Kendra's nerves were starting to get a little frayed. In the gathering gloom, the house was looking anything but inviting. She had goose bumps all over her skin, and she felt oddly glad that Adam was holding her hand. If she was on her own, she'd have turned and run. As they walked slowly up the path toward the waiting house, Kendra felt her heart starting to pound. There was nothing physical she could point to, but there was an air of gathering

17

terror about the place. She couldn't help feeling that she was making a big mistake.

They were on the porch now, and then Josh grabbed the door handle. Kendra wanted to back off and run out. The feeling of horror was growing as the light faded. She realized that Adam must be feeling something, because his palm was getting sweaty. Neither Josh nor Nicky seemed to be at all bothered, though. Josh opened the door and peered inside, grinning.

"No spooks home?" he called out in a deep, echoing voice, then laughed. "I guess they're all out dating, too. Come on, guys."

Feeling like she was walking into the jaws of a tiger, Kendra allowed Adam to lead her inside. The door closed behind them with an ominous *click*. Trying not to shiver, Kendra looked around the entrance hall.

It was very large, with a corridor leading to a stairway ahead of them. There were doors to either side of the hall, and a passageway leading off in either direction just before the stairs. There was a hat rack inside the door, and a mirror beside it. A small table and a couple of chairs were by the wall. There were paintings of landscapes on the walls, and small brackets that looked as if they might hold lamps.

It almost looked like a normal house. Only one thing was out of place.

On the floor about six feet inside the door was

Nathan's backpack. It had been dropped there, unopened. Josh frowned, realizing that something was wrong. Why would Nathan leave such an obvious clue right there by the door? Finally letting go of Nicky's hand, Josh bent to pick up the backpack.

"This is Nathan's," he muttered, and then dropped it with a start. His eyes wide and scared, he held up his hand. It was dark and sticky from where he'd touched the bag.

"Blood," he whispered, shaken.

CHAPTER 3

Kendra shuddered as she stared at Josh. The feeling of horror was growing within her. Something had gone very wrong with what was supposed to have been just a dumb joke on Adam.

"Oh, right," said Adam. "Nathan's blood. I'll just bet it is."

Kendra turned to look at him and saw that his face had clouded over—not with fear, but with anger, and he was staring not at Josh but at her. She found herself blushing without knowing why.

"So this whole thing was just a game?" Adam snapped, still looking directly at her. "You didn't *really* like me and want to date me. It was nothing more than a stupid joke, wasn't it?"

Kendra's feelings of fear were lost in her guilt and shame now. "What do you mean?" she asked.

Adam pointed down at the floor, where Josh had dropped the backpack. The pack had opened slightly, spilling some of the contents. There was a can of luminous paint, and one of those fake severed hands that wiggles around, along with a very plastic-looking bat. "What's wrong?" asked Adam angrily. "Didn't have time to plant the rest of it? When I heard Nathan Forrester's name, it all clicked. That jerk loves to play dumb jokes on people, and I guess I'm the idiot for almost falling for this one."

Still blushing, Kendra tried to regain her composure. "It was just going to be a joke," she said weakly.

Adam gave her a disgusted look. "How *could* you?" he asked. "I really thought you liked me."

"I *do*," she protested. "It was just a joke. The others talked me into it."

"Brilliant," Adam muttered. "Well, thanks a lot, Kendra. At least you've opened my eyes and shown me what you're *really* like—a silly girl who goes along with whatever her dumb friends suggest. I thought you had a mind of your own, but obviously I was wrong."

Kendra's face went even redder. Part of this was from anger—how *dare* he insult her like that! But most of it was from shame, because she knew in her heart that he was absolutely right. She *had* been dumb to allow herself to be talked into this. Before she could make her mind up about what

21

she wanted to reply, Josh gave a sort of strangled cry.

"You're wrong!" he gasped, holding up his hand. "This isn't part of the gag. It's *real* blood."

"Give it up," Adam advised him. "You can't fool me now. Your stupid game is over, get it?" He turned to go to the door. "Thanks a lot, Kendra. Not."

"No!" Josh insisted, thrusting his hand out. He looked as if he wished he could cut it off and throw it away. "Look!"

Adam hesitated, obviously bothered by Josh's intensity. Then he bent to examine Josh's stiff hand. Frowning, he knelt down and touched the backpack. His hand came up smeared and sticky. Wiping it off with a tissue, he said, suddenly very serious, "You're right, Josh. It *is* blood."

Nicole jumped. "You mean it's *not* a gag?" she squealed. "It's somebody's blood?"

Adam nodded. "At a guess, I'd say it was Nathan's."

Shivering, Kendra felt the terror taking root in her body again. Things must have gone very wrong. What had happened to Nathan? "He came in here around four," she said softly. "If the blood's still wet, something must have happened to him pretty recently, right?"

"It doesn't make sense," Adam answered. "If he'd been here for two hours then why aren't any of his stupid tricks up? But the blood *is* fresh."

22

"Then where is he?" asked Kendra. There wasn't a sign of movement in the hallway apart from their shaking. Nor was there a sound.

"I don't care!" Nicky said, her voice quavering. "This place gives me the spooks! Let's get out of here!"

Adam gave her a disgusted look. "I thought *I* was the one who was supposed to get scared here," he scoffed. "Try and grow a little backbone. Nathan must be hurt, and he might be unconscious and need a doctor. We've got to find him."

"No we don't," Nicky protested. "We don't have any lights or anything, and this place is getting really dark. Let's get out of here and call the police."

Kendra was annoyed with her friend. She didn't blame Nicky for being scared: this house was getting more and more bizarre all the time. But Nicky didn't have to wimp out so fast. "Adam's right," she said as firmly as she could. "Nathan may need help. We can't just leave him here."

"Maybe you can't," Nicky snapped. "But I can."

Kendra grabbed her friend's arm, but Adam stopped her. "No," he said gently. "The three of us can look for Nathan. Maybe it would be best if Nicole went and called for help." Kendra could see his unspoken thought: *We don't need to have to watch her while we hunt.*

23

"Yeah, right," Nicky said quickly. "That's what I meant all along. I'm not running out, I'm running for help."

Sure you are, thought Kendra bitterly. Nicole was turning out to be a real loser. Kendra felt sickened by Nicky's wimping out. "Go on then," she snapped.

Nicole didn't need a second chance. She threw herself at the door, twisting the handle so hard she could have pulled it off.

Nothing happened. The door stayed shut. Nicole tried again, rattling the door, with the same results. She turned back to them, her eyes wide and her face white. "It's no good!" she gasped. "I can't open it! The door's locked! We're trapped in here!"

24

CHAPTER 4

"What?" asked Josh, his own voice panicky. He pushed Nicole aside and shook the handle, without success. "She's right. It *is* locked!"

"It can't be," Kendra said, puzzled as much as scared by this. "It was unlocked when we came in."

"Well, it's locked now!" Nicky yelled, her voice shaking.

Adam frowned. "Maybe it's Nathan," he suggested. "He might have gone outside and locked the door on us somehow."

"Nathan!" screamed Nicky, pounding on the door with her fists. "If you did this, I swear I'm going to tear your eyeballs out!"

There was no answer from outside. Nicole started to hammer on the door again, but Kendra roughly grabbed her wrist.

25

"Knock it off," she said. "It's doing no good, and you're giving me a headache."

"We've got to get out of here!" Nicky insisted, wide-eyed. "This place really *is* haunted."

"Well, we *can't* get out," snapped Adam. "However it was done, that door is locked. And that doesn't mean this place is haunted. Come on, Nicole. Try being brave."

Kendra sighed. They weren't going to get any help from Nicky, that was certain. Nicky was on the verge of a screaming attack. "Now what do we do?" she asked Adam.

He shrugged. "What we were going to do anyway," he suggested. "Look for Nathan. If he's not in the house, then we'll *know* he's the one who locked the door."

Glancing around the darkening hallway, Kendra nodded. "But how are we going to search?" she asked. "We need light."

She saw the flash of Adam's smile even in the low light. "I bet I know where to find it," he said. Carefully avoiding the blood, he picked up the backpack and turned it over. A bunch of silly toys and tricks fell out: faintly glowing cloth ghosts, more fake bats, extra paint, and a few cans of fake intestines.

And a flashlight.

Adam snatched it up and clicked it on. A strong beam of light instantly illuminated the corridor and made Kendra blink. "All right," she said,

26

feeling slightly better. "So, where do we start looking?"

"This place hasn't been lived in for ages," Adam said. "We should be able to see Nathan's footprints in the dust without a problem." He turned the beam on the floor.

Kendra felt a chill. There were no footprints, not even their own. The reason was that there wasn't any dust. "That's weird," she muttered.

"No dust?" asked Josh. He sounded scared. "How come?"

Crossing to the hat rack, Kendra wiped her finger down the wood. There was no dust there, either. "Maybe they have a maid service?" she joked feebly.

Adam snorted, but it was good-natured. *"Somebody* has cleaned this place," he agreed. "And pretty recently, too." He shook his head. "But nobody lives here."

"Maybe it's ghosts," Nicky whimpered, her back pressed firmly against the front door. "It *must* be."

Adam snorted again. "I thought ghosts *liked* dust," he objected. "Aren't haunted houses supposed to be all cobwebs and dust?"

An idea suddenly struck Kendra. "Maybe this place isn't abandoned after all," she suggested. "Maybe crooks are using it to hide their loot in, knowing that people never come here. If Nathan found them, they might have..." Her voice trailed off. She didn't want to finish that thought.

"Hurt him?" Adam suggested, tactfully. He shook his head. "Then why would they leave his bag lying here?"

"Well, what do you think happened?" demanded Josh.

"I don't know," Adam replied. "But the easiest way to find out is to find Nathan. So let's start looking." He gave a slight smile. "The best way to search would be for us to split up," he said. "But ..." He didn't need to say any more.

"No way," Kendra said firmly. "There's only one flashlight, and I'm going where it goes."

"I'm not going any further into this house!" Nicky said wildly. "It's too scary. I'm staying right here!"

"Smart move," said Adam. "You stay here, nice and safe in the dark, all alone. We'll pick you up on the way back."

Kendra couldn't help laughing at the thought. Nicky had asked for it. As the idea sunk in, Nicky gave a cry and leaped forward, clutching at Josh's hand. "Okay," she said, shivering. "I'll come with you guys."

"What a surprise," muttered Kendra. She was wondering again why she'd ever wanted to be friends with the blond girl. She was turning out to be a real pain in the butt. Okay, this house was definitely spooky and some really bizarre

28

things were happening, but screaming and moaning wouldn't help.

"Right," said Adam. "Now that we agree, let's stay close and move out." He shone the beam of light onto the closest door on the left. "Kendra, you open the door carefully—if it will open—and I'll shine the light inside. If it's okay, I'll lead the way in." He glanced at Nicole. "You bring up the rear." Positioning himself directly in front of the door, he pointed the beam on the handle. "Ready?"

Kendra swallowed, fighting down feelings of panic. She had to stay calm until they found Nathan and got out of this place. Her hand was shaking as she reached for the handle, but she forced herself to stay as calm as possible. Gripping the handle, she gave it a sudden jerk down, and then threw the door wide open.

The beam from the flashlight illuminated the whole room in a second. Kendra was ready to run or to scream, or *anything* if something moved. Nothing did, however, so Adam pushed gently past her and into the room. She followed quickly, and the other two slid nervously in behind them.

This was some kind of lounge. There were several high-back, plush armchairs, and two small tables. Several bookshelves lined the walls, each filled with hardcovers. There were more paintings on the walls, and brackets for lights. In the center of the room was a large chandelier, hanging from the ceiling. Crystal or glass glittered in the beam from the flashlight.

On the left-hand wall, which would be the front of the house, there was a set of thick drapes, closed now. But no sign of Nathan. And, once again, the room looked clean, neat, and dusted— not abandoned and decayed. What was going on in this place?

"Nothing," said Adam, sounding disappointed. "Well, let's try the next room."

"No, wait!" exclaimed Nicky. She pointed at the drapes. "There's a window. If we open that, we can get out."

"We don't want to get out," Kendra said. "Well, not yet."

"I do," Nicky said. She crossed to the rope pull that was at the side of the drapes. She gave it a tug. Swishing slightly, the drapes opened, showing that beyond them was a bay window. Nothing could be seen outside the glass; it was total blackness.

"That can't be right," muttered Josh. "We should at least be able to see the streetlights out there."

"Yeah," agreed Adam. He shone the flashlight at the glass, and frowned. It was as if the light wouldn't go through the glass. The beam stopped dead when it hit the window. "That's really weird."

"I don't care!" Nicky yelled. She sounded as if

she were on the verge of hysterics. "I'm going out that window if I have to throw a chair through it!" She jumped up onto the wide ledge and fumbled with the catch. To Kendra's surprise, it opened almost soundlessly. Somebody had to be taking care of things in this house.

And then she just stared at what lay outside the window. With the glass open, Adam was able to shine the flashlight outside and they could all see what lay out there. And it wasn't the garden they had come through to get into the house.

It was a jungle—literally. There were towering trees whose tops they couldn't see in the darkness. There were creepers hanging from branches, and even large, exotic flowers that looked washed out and pale in the beam of the light. Soft, chittering noises and an occasional birdcall broke the silence of the night, along with the humming of locusts and other nocturnal insects.

Josh grabbed hold of Nicole's arm. "You're not going out there!" he exclaimed. "I don't know what's going on, but that's got to be half a world away from home!"

"It's better than staying in this house a second longer," Nicky replied, struggling to get free.

"You've got to be kidding!" Kendra snapped. She gestured out at the jungle. "That's *impossible.* It can't really be there!"

"And you'd have to be really stupid to want to go out there," added Adam scornfully.

31

"I'm—" began Nicky, still trying to break free of Josh's grip. Then she stared out into the jungle and screamed.

Caught squarely in the beam from Adam's flashlight was a huge, bestial face. Kendra jumped back as she realized that it was a lion or something—a huge, teeth-filled mouth that suddenly opened in a warning roar.

With two huge, saberlike fangs hanging down . . .

The saber-toothed tiger coiled, then sprang straight at them.

CHAPTER 5

Nicky screamed and jumped back from the window, sending Josh and herself sprawling to the floor in a squealing, hysterical knot.

Kendra and Adam both reacted together. Not even thinking of the danger, Kendra's only thought was to keep the tiger outside. She grabbed the open window and slammed it down. Adam had obviously had the same idea, and he helped her latch it.

Would the thin glass stand up to the attack? Or would the tiger smash through and into the room, where they would be trapped with it?

There was a huge crash as the beast slammed into the outside of the window. Kendra was ready to join Nicky in screaming at the top of her lungs. The monster was going to get in and rip them all to shreds!

But the glass didn't break. Instead, she heard the tiger fall back to the ground outside. Then came another slamming noise. It must have hit the window with a paw. It roared in rage and frustration. But it wasn't able to get in!

Kendra felt her whole body relaxing as the shock and fear left her. "We're safe in here," she whispered.

Adam gave her an odd, lopsided grin. "That's a strange way of putting it," he told her. "We're *trapped* in here, remember?"

"Yes," she agreed, refusing to let go of the good mood that had suddenly filled her when the tiger couldn't break in. "But at least *it's* not trapped in here with us."

"Be thankful for small favors?" asked Adam. Then he stared down at Nicky and Josh, who had finally stopped screaming. *They were probably too hoarse,* Kendra thought. "Well," Adam said, "you two were a big help." He kicked Josh gently on the thigh. "Come on, get up." He glared at Nicky. "You still want to go out that window?"

"No way!" she squealed, clambering to her feet. She brushed her messy curls from her eyes. Kendra saw how wide and terrified they were. "I'd be killed."

"You almost were," Kendra said coldly. "Why didn't you do something instead of just freaking out like that?"

"I was *scared stiff,*" Nicky protested.

34

"We all were," Kendra replied. "But if Adam and I hadn't slammed that window, we'd be dead." She felt as disgusted with Nicole and Joshua as Adam did. "Try and pull yourself together."

"Yes," Adam added. "There's no telling what dangers lay in store. I don't think my ears can take any more of your screams, and we could use your help."

"You think . . ." Josh asked, gulping. "You think there are *more* problems?"

"Use your brains," suggested Adam. "We can't get out the front door, and now we don't dare try the windows. Whatever is out there"—he gestured at the glass with his flashlight—"it isn't Forrester, is it? And I don't care how big a practical joker Nathan is, there's no way he could have faked that sabertooth."

Kendra frowned. Adam was right. She'd been too scared and then too relieved to think about what they had seen. Slowly, she added, "Then that can't even be just some jungle thousands of miles from home. Saber-tooth tigers have been extinct for thousands of years."

"What are you saying?" asked Josh. He looked scared enough to start puking any second. "What is it out there?"

"I don't know," Kendra told him. "But if this *is* a haunted house, that was too solid a ghost for my liking."

35

Adam shook his head. "I don't think that was any ghost," he said slowly. "I've heard of animal ghosts, but they're usually dogs or cats—pets, creatures that are used to being around people. Nothing like a saber-toothed tiger. Anyway, I heard the crickets out in that forest, and I could smell the plants and everything. That was *way* too real to be any kind of spook."

Kendra didn't like the way this conversation was going. "You don't mean that you think that what we saw was *real,* do you?"

"What other choice is there?" Adam asked simply. "One, it was real, somehow. Two, it was a hallucination. Three, it was a haunting. Four, it was a trick of some kind." He grimaced. "I think we can rule out the trick. There's no way Nathan could manage anything like that. As for the haunting—well, maybe. But like I said, it's the strangest sort of ghost I've ever heard of. A hallucination? All four of us seeing the same thing? And a mirage that can rattle windows? I don't think so. That leaves only number one: somehow, what we saw was real."

There was a moment of stunned silence, then Nicole started to whimper: "I want to go home."

"We all do," said Kendra, trying to be sympathetic. "But crying isn't going to make it happen. So pull yourself together."

Nicole stared at her in shock. "How can you

36

say that?" she asked, tears welling up in her eyes. "You're supposed to be my friend."

"Well, I just quit," snapped Kendra. "I've had enough of your whining, so knock it off." She deliberately turned her back on Nicky and faced Adam. "Now what?"

"I guess we try the next room," Adam replied. "And just expect the unexpected." He managed a wan smile. "I think that this house still has more surprises for us up its sleeves."

"Yeah," agreed Kendra. "That's what I'm afraid of."

Adam led the way to the door again, and opened it. That made Kendra frown. She didn't recall any of them closing it behind them when they entered the room. This house seemed to have a habit of somehow closing its own doors.

As Adam stepped into the corridor, he stopped dead. Kendra banged into him, and scowled.

"What—" she started, and then broke off. The reason he'd halted was quite obvious.

In all of the light fixtures down the hall, tall white candles were now lit and burning, throwing a cheery glow over the hall that sent shivers down her spine.

"We're not alone in here," Adam said, stating the obvious.

37

CHAPTER 6

"I don't like this house one bit," muttered Kendra, struggling not to panic.

"Me either," agreed Adam. Surprisingly, he reached out and gave her hand a reassuring squeeze. "You're holding up well, though."

Kendra didn't know what to say. It felt nice to have him approve of her. Instead, she nodded at the candles. "Why would anyone light them?" she asked.

"Because it's getting too dark to see?" he suggested.

"So whoever it is can see *us*," gasped Nicole. "It's probably some maniac with an ax, wanting to kill us. Like he's already killed Nathan!" She was breathing in short, panicky gasps.

"We don't know that Nathan's dead," Kendra

pointed out. "And with those candles lit, we could see any mad killer just as easily as he could see us." She really didn't want to consider the thought that Nicky could be right. But it was all too tempting . . . *Something* had happened to Nathan, and whatever it had been had left his blood on the backpack.

"If anyone had hacked Nathan to death," Adam objected, "I think there would have been a lot more blood. Plus, probably, dripping body parts." He frowned. "You know, I think that these candles are meant to be helpful." He clicked off the flashlight and slipped it into his coat pocket. "I mean, now we can see okay."

Kendra shook her head. "This place is getting weirder all the time. Okay, we *know* there's somebody here. Why won't they show themselves?"

"I saw this TV show once," Josh said, his voice low and scared. "There was an old guy who lived alone in a house that was supposed to be deserted. He hid out all the time because he was awfully deformed, and people would scream just by looking at him. Maybe *that's* what's happening here."

"Life isn't like TV shows," Kendra objected. "If it was, I'd move to Beverly Hills right now."

"That doesn't mean he's entirely wrong," Adam argued. "It's possible that someone *does* live here who doesn't want to be seen for some reason."

39

"Oh, great," said Nicole, shaking. "So you want us to walk around this house while somebody we can't see lurks in the shadows, just waiting for us?"

Adam glared at her. "I don't think we have a whole lot of choice in the matter, do we? If you don't want to come with us, then you can stay here on your own. At least you'll be able to see anyone who attacks you."

Nicole glared furiously back at him. "Why are you being so mean to me?" she demanded. "I just want a little sympathy."

"Then get it from your boyfriend," Adam replied. "Why can't you be more like Kendra?" Without waiting for an answer, he strode to the next door on the left. "Okay, who's with me?"

Wondering what would lie behind door number two, Kendra went after him. She heard Nicole and Joshua scuttle quickly behind her. The thought of being left alone obviously terrified them more than exploring another room. Adam smiled grimly, then winked at Kendra. She felt better knowing that he seemed to be forgiving her. And, come to think of it, he was rather good-looking. He was certainly brighter and braver than either Josh or Nathan.

Adam opened the door, and they all gasped at what met their eyes.

The room beyond was lit by another of the gorgeous glass chandeliers hanging from the ceiling.

40

This one had something like a hundred lit candles in it, all casting their glow through the sparkling glass and onto the room below. It was obviously a formal dining room. In the center of the room was a large, polished wooden table, with a dozen chairs arranged around it. Against the walls were the hutches and sideboards that must hold all of the dishes and silverware. There were more pictures on the walls, and several smaller tables scattered about, each with large, covered silver dishes on them.

The most amazing thing, though, was that the table was set . . . for four people. There were fresh napkins in silver swan-shaped napkin rings; large bone-china plates, with a delicate floral pattern; and water glasses, each filled almost to the brim.

And there were steaming platters on the table in front of the plates. One held a large roast beef, and another a small ham. Kendra wandered slowly over to the table. The dishes held Brussels sprouts, carrots and peas, and roasted potatoes. There was a steaming dish of gravy, and a plate of pineapple chunks. It looked and smelled absolutely delicious. Her stomach rumbled slightly, reminding her that she hadn't eaten since lunch.

"How could anyone have done all this without us hearing them?" she asked softly. This was the spookiest thing yet: to have cooked this meal and laid it out in this room—and with the lights having

41

been lit only moments earlier? There were only two doors into this room, and they had entered through one. There had been no sign of anyone in the hall.

"And *why?*" asked Adam, just as puzzled. He moved forward, and sniffed hard. "This is making my mouth water," he confessed. "I *hate* Brussels sprouts, though. Why couldn't it be burgers and fries?"

"It might be poisoned!" Nicole gasped in horror.

"I wasn't going to try it," Adam answered, looking as if he wished he could. "But I don't think anyone would cook a meal like this just to poison us with it. It doesn't make a lot of sense."

"Nothing much in this house makes sense," complained Kendra. "This is just—if you'll forgive me—the icing on the cake. I don't get it. One second, something's scaring us to death. The next second, they're laying out a banquet for us."

"I still think it's poisoned!" Nicole insisted. "Whoever is in this house is trying to kill us. That food is just another trap."

"Who do you think we are?" snapped Kendra. "Hansel and Gretel? Give me a break." But she didn't want to be the first to try the food. She might be hungry, and it might smell really tempting. But she wasn't stupid, and she wasn't suicidal. Reluctantly, she tore her gaze away from the table.

There was a second door out of the room to her right. The one that they had entered by was behind her. She glanced over her shoulder and saw that it was closed. That was getting to be a pattern of some kind, at least. On the far side of the room were more of the floor-length drapes. Kendra pointed at them. "Want to see what lies outside window number two?" she asked.

Nicole shuddered. "I . . . think I'll stay inside for now."

"Smart decision," approved Adam. "So . . . let's see what's beyond that door, shall we?" He gave a last, lingering, regretful look at the table and then marched over to the other door. Kendra, Josh, and Nicole followed him across the room and watched as he threw open the door.

The room beyond was obviously the kitchen. It was fairly large, and in many ways quite old-fashioned. There was a large, dark oven that seemed to be fueled by burning logs. Beside it was a stack of cut wood, ready for loading. A large sink, and a huge butcher-block table stood in the center of the room, and there were large, free-standing cupboards, with several racks holding fresh, uncooked vegetables.

Again, there was no sign of anyone.

"Notice something very strange?" Adam asked quietly.

"In *this* house?" replied Kendra, almost

amused enough to laugh. "Adam, *everything* here is strange."

"True, but I meant something really puzzling." He gestured all around. "That food on the table in the other room is piping hot, and must just have been cooked. Yet there isn't a single dirty pan. And that stove looks cold to me."

Kendra crossed to it and touched it quickly, in case she burned herself.

Nothing happened. It was almost as cold as ice.

"But this is impossible," she said. "If the food's just been cooked, *where* was it cooked? It couldn't have been in here . . . but it couldn't have been anywhere else."

"I think I'm getting too much strangeness in one dose," Adam answered. "It's getting to be expected, instead of unusual."

"But it's still scary," Kendra said. "This whole place is just too weird for me." She sighed. "I guess we try another room now, right?"

"What else can we do?" asked Adam. "So far, there's been no sign of either Nathan or anyone else living."

"And no way out," complained Josh.

"Yeah, I know," sighed Kendra. "You want to go home." She crossed to one of the kitchen's other doors. "This one should lead out back," she guessed. "That other one back there will lead to the hallway, I suppose." She stopped with her

44

hand on the handle. "What will happen when I try this?" she asked.

"There's no way to know until you do," Adam replied. "But I should be the one to try it first."

"Why?" snapped Kendra. "Because you're a guy? Or because you've got a death wish?" She refused to allow him to be the bravest of them all constantly. "Too late." Gripping the handle, she twisted it as hard as she could, prepared for almost anything.

CHAPTER 7

And absolutely nothing happened. The handle refused to move.

Kendra gave another sigh. "It looks as if we're still trapped in here," she said. "This door's just as stuck as the front door." She glanced at the window over the sink. There were no curtains covering it, but only blackness could be seen beyond. "Anyone want to try the window?"

Nicky shuddered at the thought. Josh shook his head emphatically.

Adam shrugged. "Then I guess it's back to the hall, and we try the rooms on the far side of the corridor." He gave Kendra a small smile. "You don't mind if I lead, do you?"

She shrugged. "I guess it's your turn to risk your neck first." She wasn't going to tell him that

46

she liked him smiling at her. Besides, what would Nicky think?

Then again, who *cared* what Nicky thought?

They left the kitchen and found themselves in the corridor again. Kendra glanced at the stairs, but they had to finish checking the ground-floor first. She wasn't sure what lay upstairs, but she was willing to bet it wouldn't be anything as simple or as safe as empty bedrooms.

There were just two doors on the far side of the hallway. With a shrug, Adam strode back to the one closest to the front door, and then opened it. The others followed him through and into the room beyond. It turned out that the other door also led here into this huge room.

It was obviously a library and family room. Bookcases lined all of the walls, from floor to ceiling. Only on the south wall was there a break in the cases. It had a small fireplace, with the logs laid ready. There was even one of those stepladders with wheels that enabled one to reach the top shelves. Kendra had no idea how many books were here, but it must have been over a thousand. They were all neatly shelved and dusted, save for two. One of those was on a large, brass lectern that was shaped like an eagle with its wings spread. The book rested on the open wings. Kendra glanced at it, and saw that it was one of those huge, old-fashioned family bibles.

That gave her an idea. Her great-grandparents

had owned one of these, and they had used the back pages to record the family tree. Maybe whoever owned this house had done the same. She carefully turned the pages to the back and then examined what had been handwritten there.

The first entry was a Jeremiah Hawkins, born in 1492—the year America had been discovered!—and who died in 1571. There were lists of children, but she didn't want to read every entry. There were two pages of them, and she turned the page over for the final entry.

It was for a Jeremiah Clarke, and he was listed as being born in 1754. There was no date of death, and no entry after this one.

And it looked as if it had been written in very recently . . .

Shivering, she turned to examine the rest of the room. She didn't even want to think about what she had discovered—if she had really found out anything. There could be lots of reasons why there hadn't been any further entries.

There was a large, old-fashioned desk over by one of the large windows, with a large inkpot and several old quill pens on it. Adam was examining these. He took the lid off the pot and blinked. "Hey, there's fresh ink in here!" he exclaimed.

"Who cares?" complained Nicky. "It doesn't help us to get out of here. It's just another dumb thing that's happened."

Kendra had to stop herself from growling at her

48

one-time friend. Still, Nicky was right. Another mystery wouldn't help make things any clearer. She finished examining the room. There were several large, high-backed, padded chairs. They'd be comfortable to sit in to read. Each chair had a small table beside it. One of them had an open book laid out. Curiosity got the best of her and she crossed to see what the book was.

She gave a slight start. It was Mark Twain's *Life on the Mississippi.* "Weird," she muttered. "I was just reading this at home earlier." Then she felt all the color drain from her face. It was open to page 103 . . . exactly where she'd stopped reading before Adam had arrived . . . "This is just *too* weird," she complained. Was it possible that whoever was organizing whatever was going on somehow knew what she'd been reading, and what page she was up to? But how?

Josh and Nicole were standing by a small chess table on a stand. The pieces were set up as if a game was under way, with some of the pieces on the shelf under the board. "It's like people were here just a short while ago," Josh muttered. "And they just stepped out or something."

"Not out of these doors," Nicky snapped. "Nobody can get through any of them."

"This isn't getting us anywhere," Adam said. "Aside from the windows behind the drapes, there's no other way out of this room. I guess we'll have to try upstairs next."

"Maybe not," said Nicky slowly. She was staring at a lit hurricane lamp on the desk. "Maybe there's another way out of this place."

"What do you mean?" Kendra asked, puzzled.

Nicole pointed at the lamp. "That thing has oil in it. Maybe we can't break open the front door, but I'll bet we could use that lamp to *burn* through."

Adam looked appalled. "Have you totally flipped?" he demanded. "If you start a fire in this house with all the doors locked, all you'll do is kill us."

Nicole glared at him, grimacing. "Well, has anyone else got a better idea?" she demanded. "None of you have *any* ideas to get us out of here, do you?" She glared at Kendra and then at Adam. "You two are acting like this is just a class trip to the zoo or something. We're *trapped* in here, and we've got to get out. And I'll do whatever I have to in order to escape."

She snatched up the lantern, and then dashed for the door. Kendra and Adam were on the far side of the room, but they rushed after her. Josh simply stood there, his mouth open and his face in shock.

Kendra saw in horror that Nicky was too far away to be stopped. She was in the hallway, and raising the lamp to throw it with all her force at the door. "Nicky!" she screamed. "Don't do it! You'll get us all killed!"

But she knew she was too late.

50

CHAPTER
8

As Nicky was about to throw the lamp at the door, there suddenly came a terrified scream from upstairs. It was clearly from someone in a great deal of pain and fear. Worse, Kendra recognized the voice: it was Nathan.

The horrifying sound froze Nicky in her tracks, and then she turned around slowly to stare at the stairs. As she did so, Adam reached her and grabbed the lamp from her shaking fingers before she could throw it—or more likely drop it.

"Did you hear that?" Nicky asked, shaking, and pointing with a trembling finger. "It came from upstairs."

"Yes," agreed Kendra, relieved that Adam now had the lamp. He placed it carefully out of Nicole's reach on one of the tables in the hall. "I'm sure it was Nathan's voice." She shuddered. "He's still alive, then."

"And in trouble," Adam added, starting for the stairs. "Well, don't just stand there—we have to go help him. Even if he is a rat."

"Up there?" asked Nicky.

"Let's not go through all this again," Kendra snapped. She grabbed the other girl's wrist tightly and dragged her along. "We're staying together, so stop complaining." Josh brought up the rear, pale and sweating.

To Kendra's surprise, the stairs didn't give a single squeak as they went up. This house was *definitely* in much better condition than it had any right to be. At the top of the stairs, Adam hesitated. There was just a single corridor leading back toward the front of the house. There were four doors off each side of this corridor, and a large window at the end that presumably looked out over the front of the house. Except, like all the other windows, there was nothing to be seen through it.

"We'll start with the first room on the left," Adam decided. "Stick close together. Something obviously scared Nathan." He opened the door.

As with the other rooms, there were candles burning inside this one. It was a bedroom, obviously. There was a large four-poster bed with curtains that were tied back to show that the bed was freshly made and turned down. It looked as if someone might get into it at any moment. There was a closet in the corner, and a dressing table. On the table was a jug and a bowl, for washing in. Kendra frowned. That had gone out of fashion a hundred years ago! Adam crossed to the closet and flung the door open. Inside it hung girl's clothing, but it all looked antique in style. There were long dresses and coats and even petticoats. Yet it also looked absolutely brand-new.

And, even weirder, her size . . .

"He's not here," Josh pointed out.

"Then we try the next room," Adam shot back. "Come on." They went next door, to discover another bedroom like the first. Only in the closet here were ancient-looking clothes for a boy— again brand-new. And they looked as if they might fit Adam or Josh. Kendra didn't like the implications of that. Could it be pure coincidence that the clothing they'd found was the right size to fit them all? And what about the book in the library? And the food on the table? This was getting way too creepy for her.

The third room on the left was an old-fashioned bathroom, with a large metal tub and a big radiator. The closet was loaded with fresh towels. There was even soap by the tub, and bath crystals that smelled very fresh.

But still no sign of life.

The final room on the left was another bedroom. This one had a much larger four-poster bed, though, and two closets. The clothing in these were still the same hundred-years-out-of-date stuff, but in adult sizes.

Did these clothes belong to whoever lived here? But if they did, why did it look so old-fashioned? The more that they discovered in this place, the less sense any of it made.

The opposite room on the right-hand side of the corridor was a storage room, filled with trunks and shelves full of bric-a-brac. There were model sailing ships, pressed flowers, stuffed animals and birds—some of which Kendra was certain were extinct, like a large dodo. Adam opened one of the trunks, which contained old games and other odd stuff. Again, there was no sign of anyone there.

The next three rooms were all bedrooms, like the first ones that they had examined. In these, though, the closets were bare. In none of the rooms was there any sign of Nathan.

"Do you think there's an attic?" Kendra asked Adam.

He looked up at the ceiling. "Maybe," he said uncertainly. "But I haven't seen any way to get into one. And we all heard Nathan scream. It was too loud to have come from the attic. So where *is* he?"

"Do you think he's hiding?" suggested Josh. "Maybe he really is playing a trick on all of us."

"His scream was too real," Adam answered.

"He sounded terrified and in pain. Nathan's not a good enough actor to fake that."

"Then where *is* he?" demanded Nicky. "We've been through every room in the house now. There isn't anywhere else to look."

"I know," agreed Adam, puzzled. "He doesn't seem to be in the house at all."

An idea suddenly struck Kendra. "Maybe he *isn't* in the house."

Adam frowned. "What do you mean?"

"I mean that maybe he went out of the house," Kendra explained. "Like Nicky tried to do— through one of the windows."

"Into that jungle?" Adam shuddered. "He wouldn't last five minutes in that."

"Besides," objected Josh, "if he'd gone out of a window, then it would still be open, wouldn't it? And they were all closed."

Kendra snorted. "Haven't you been paying attention?" she asked. "Whenever we go through a door, it closes behind us. Maybe the windows in this house do the same sort of thing."

"On their own?" asked Josh.

Adam shrugged. "Maybe that's the way they're built. To save energy or something. But Kendra's right. Since we know Nathan isn't in the house, he *must* have gone out somehow."

"Then let's check," Kendra suggested, pointing at the bedroom window. "We're on the first floor. I don't think that saber-toothed tiger could jump up this high. It should be fairly safe to check outside and see if we can spot Nathan."

"I'm game," agreed Adam. They went to the window. Nicky and Josh simply clutched at each other and remained in the center of the room. Chickens!

Adam took a deep breath and tugged up the window. It opened effortlessly, and light streamed in from outside.

It was bright daylight out there! This was utterly impossible! And as Kendra peered out, she saw something even more impossible.

It wasn't the jungle out there. It wasn't even the overgrown garden that they had entered the house through.

There was a rolling meadow, with clumps of trees that stretched as far as she could see. It looked like early spring, not the late fall. The ground was pocked with craters, and as she stared out in disbelief, there came the unmistakable sounds of guns being fired.

CHAPTER 9

"Guns ..." Kendra gasped as they all dived to the floor. The *pop-pop* sounds continued every few moments.

"Not quite," Adam said, puzzled. "That's not *modern* gunfire. It sounds like muskets to me." When Kendra looked at him oddly, he grinned. "My dad's a gun nut," he explained. "He took me to one of those historical reenactments. The sound of musket fire is unmistakable."

"So who cares *what* they're shooting?" howled Nicole. "They're still trying to kill us!"

"I don't think so," Adam said. He was crouched by the open window, and he glanced over the edge.

"Be careful!" Kendra exclaimed, worried for him.

"It's okay," he told her. "They're not firing in this direction. I can see the puffs of smoke from some of the muskets." Kendra rose slowly next to him to gaze out of the window. He gestured to the north. "There's one group of them up there," he said. Sure enough, a few seconds later Kendra saw puffs of smoke and heard the sound of popping. He gestured to the south. "That's where the others are. They're firing at each other."

"I don't get it," Kendra muttered. "What's going on out there?"

"It's a battle," Adam explained. "Every now and then you can see the ones in the north are wearing red when one of them stands up."

This wasn't making any sense to her. "In our sleepy little town?" she asked. "Adam, they don't even have *fights,* let alone gun battles."

"Not now," he agreed. "But they did in 1778. The British overran the area, and the Patriots had to retreat. Don't you pay attention in history?" But he said this quite kindly, so she wasn't offended.

"But that was . . ." she gasped.

"Two hundred or more years ago," agreed Adam.

"You mean that they're *ghosts* out there, reliving the battle?" asked Josh. He was pale again, and shivering.

"I don't think so," Adam said. "For one thing,

58

there're dozens of soldiers out there. That would be an awful lot of ghosts in one spot, wouldn't it? For another—it's *daylight* out there. And in this room it's night. There's something going on here that's *much* weirder than a haunting."

Kendra was starting to catch on. "It's like time outside the house is being changed somehow," she said slowly. "That prehistoric jungle, and now this battle that was fought over two hundred years ago."

"Right," agreed Adam, giving her an encouraging smile. "You're as smart as you're pretty. And time *inside* the house is just as odd. Like the kitchen being clean even though the meal was hot in the dining room." He pointed to one of the candles in the room. "And the fact that the candles are all burning, but they're not melting. It's as if time as we know it has broken down here somehow."

That made some sense to Kendra, but it wasn't at all reassuring. "So what does it *mean?*" she asked.

"I wish I knew," admitted Adam. "But at least part of it is starting to make some strange kind of sense."

"But it doesn't get us out of here," complained Nicky. "I want to go *home,* not to some battlefield or some prehistoric jungle where I'll be eaten!"

"I know," agreed Kendra. "I want to go home, too. But it's looking like it's harder to get home than we thought." She turned back to Adam. "Do you think that the front door will take us home?" she asked. "Maybe that's why it's locked."

"It could be," he agreed. "But our first priority is to find Nathan. I want to punch him in the nose for getting us into this."

"Me too," agreed Kendra. "What a jerk. I can't believe how dumb I was to agree to this." She looked at him, and swallowed all her pride. "I'm really sorry for what I did, Adam. Honest."

He grinned. "I believe you. And you're forgiven."

"I know I don't deserve it," she said slowly. "But—will you give me another chance when we get out of here? I'd really like to go out with you."

Adam grinned again, wider this time. "Definitely. Only next time I pick the place. Deal?"

"Deal," she agreed happily. For a second she almost forgot their troubles. Then a fresh outburst of firing from outside reminded her strongly of the danger they were in.

Adam peered out of the window, and then stiffened. "I think I can see Nathan," he said suddenly. He pointed to a small crater beyond a battered old wall. "There, look."

Kendra followed his lead and saw a huddled figure in the hole in the ground. He had his hands over his head, but she recognized the T-shirt and jeans Nathan had been wearing earlier. "That's him!" she agreed. "Thank goodness!"

"Well, *call* him," barked Josh. "Get him back here!"

"No," Adam replied, before anyone could. "If we call to him, the soldiers might hear us. At the moment, they're firing at each other. I don't like the thought of them discovering that we're here."

"Then what are we going to do?" asked Josh. "Just leave him there?"

"It *is* tempting," admitted Adam. "But no. I'll go out and drag him back if I have to. You guys just wait here for me, okay?"

Kendra was worried for him. She had surprised herself by growing quite fond of Adam. He was brave, bright and funny, and she really did like him now. "Be careful," she said. "You owe me a date, remember?"

"I'll be back to keep it," he promised. Then he winked and climbed over the windowsill. Kendra could see that there was a drainpipe running down the wall to the ground. He grabbed hold of it, and then used it to climb down.

Her heart was pounding as she watched him cross the small backyard to the battered wall. She couldn't help being scared for him. He was risking his own life to try and help someone he didn't even like that much. She prayed that the soldiers wouldn't spot him. In the distance, they were still firing at one another.

61

Adam clambered over the wall and then, keeping low, scuttled across to the shell hole where Nathan was cowering. Kendra saw him tap Nathan on the shoulder. Nathan almost jumped out of his skin, and looked like he might faint any second. She wasn't surprised to see that Nathan was obviously a coward. He must have run outside to try and escape from the house and then been too scared to even move. She saw Adam point back to the house, and Nathan shake his head in fear. Jeez, what a wimp! He was too scared to try and make it back. Adam argued with him for a few minutes. They were too far away for Kendra to hear anything, but she saw Adam wave a bunched-up fist under Nathan's nose, obviously threatening to punch his lights out if he didn't make the trip back.

Nathan howled in fear. They all heard him.

So did the soldiers. There was a short break in their firing, and then more of the pop-popping sounds. Kendra almost screamed as she saw bullets kick up the dirt around the boys.

The soldiers were trying to kill Adam and Nathan!

CHAPTER
10

As she watched, Kendra saw that the bullets zipping close by had finally made Nathan realize how unsafe his position was. Adam managed to get him to run for cover behind the battered wall. Kendra was relieved to see that the two boys could rest there and catch their breath. The bullets fired at them hit the stone wall instead. In a couple of minutes, they could run the rest of the way back to the house. Thankfully, once they reached it, they should be well out of firing range.

Unless the soldiers moved.

Kendra saw that a couple of red-coated men were heading in the direction of the house, keeping low to avoid being shot by the Patriots. They must assume that Adam and Nathan were part of the American forces! Kendra knew that some of the soldiers in the Revolutionary War were teenagers, so it wasn't that crazy a mistake to make.

But it could be a very deadly one for Adam and Nathan . . .

She glanced at the drainpipe that Adam had used to climb down and then stiffened in shock. It was starting to tear away from the outside wall. It had never been meant to be used as a ladder. If Adam tried to get back in that way, it would pull free, no question. And if he couldn't get back in, those redcoats would shoot him down.

Kendra didn't have time to panic. She had to act. She twisted around and glared at Nicky and Josh, who were still cowering for cover. "Get the sheets off that bed," she ordered. "We've got to make a rope ladder for Adam and Nathan. The pipe's not safe enough."

"Leave us alone," whimpered Nicky.

Kendra moved across to them. "Adam's out there risking his life for your dumb friend," she said slowly. "The least you can do is get your act together and *help*."

"I *hate* you," Nicky groaned. But she started to pull the sheets off the bed.

"Yeah, fine," Kendra replied. "Just do it."

Together the three of them tied four sheets at the corners. Kendra tested the knots, and decided that they had to hold. "Grab this end," she ordered her reluctant helpers. "And hold on tight."

Taking the rest of the linens, she returned to the window and glanced out.

Adam and Nathan were sprinting for the house now. The two redcoats had spotted them and were racing after them. It was going to be a close call! Quickly, she threw her end of the ladder out. It almost reached the ground, thank goodness! Adam was the first to reach it, but he waited for Nathan.

"Go on," he ordered, "Fast!"

Nathan didn't need any further encouragement. Grabbing the sheets, he started up. Kendra held on to the other end of the ladder with Josh and Nicky. She could hear the fabric groaning and starting to tear under the strain. But it had to hold up!

Then Nathan popped through the window and dived for cover behind the bed. Kendra risked another look out of the window as Adam started to climb. The two soldiers had stopped running and had brought their old-fashioned muskets up to their shoulders. Both guns fired. Chunks of wood were chipped out of the house's shingles, but Adam wasn't hit. Then the soldiers had to reload their rifles before they could fire again. Kendra was relieved; she'd forgotten that the older guns were single shot!

Then Adam came over the windowsill and fell to the floor beside her. "Thanks," he said, grinning. "I wondered how we were going to get back in."

"I'm glad you're safe," she said. To Nicky and Josh, she ordered, "Pull up the sheets, fast."

"Why?" Josh complained. "Just leave them."

"So those soldiers can climb up?" Kendra snapped. "We have to close this window again, or we won't be safe."

That made them move. In seconds, they had the sheets back in the room, and Adam slammed the window shut. As he did so, Kendra heard the two soldiers fire again. The bullets slammed into the glass of the window, making it rattle. But amazingly, the window didn't break under the impact.

"I think we're safe for now," Kendra said, collapsing onto the floor.

Adam couldn't resist a small smile. "Right," he agreed ironically. "We're safely trapped inside the house." He glanced over at Nathan, who was shaking on the floor behind the bed. "Return of the hero," he said mockingly.

"I've been through a lot," Nathan replied, but without his usual nastiness. He was almost whining. Just like Nicky and Josh, Kendra realized. What a bunch of losers she'd picked as friends!

"We all have," she told him. "This idea of yours to play practical jokes in a haunted house has really backfired, hasn't it?"

"How was I to know it *really* is haunted?" Nathan asked. He shuddered. "I've been scared ever since I stepped in here earlier."

Adam nodded. "So what happened to you?" he asked. "We found your backpack with blood all over it."

66

Nathan held up his right hand, which was bandaged very roughly with a strip that had been torn from the bottom of his T-shirt. "Most of it was from my hand," he explained. "It hurts a lot."

"What happened?" asked Josh.

"When I came in," he said, "the door shut behind me. I couldn't open it, so I got my knife from my bag to try and pry open the lock. Then I heard this terrible roaring noise from the side room. I opened the window to check and this small, furry thing came jumping at me. It was bleeding like crazy, and it bit me, but I fought it off and shut the window. The blood got all over me. Then I tried to escape through the bedroom window here. But it wasn't safe, either. When I was outside, those maniacs started shooting at one another. It was like I was caught in a gang war or something."

"It *was* something," Kendra informed him. "Actually, it was the Revolutionary War."

He stared at her in disbelief. "You've got to be joking."

"Practical jokes are your specialty," she replied. "I don't know how, but time in this place is all wrong. The roaring noise you heard was probably a saber-toothed tiger. We saw one from the sitting-room window. It thought Nicky was a snack."

Nicole glared at her. "Stop making jokes!" she yelled. "I can't take any more of this. This house is *evil*. I've got to get out of here!"

"We've tried that," Adam pointed out. "And

so far we've had no luck at all." He started for the door. "Still, now that we've rescued Nathan, we have to start looking for another way out. And that means going back downstairs."

As they all filed down the staircase, he looked over at Nathan. "Do you still have your knife with you? That idea of prying open the lock wasn't a bad one."

Nathan flushed. "I . . . dropped it out there in the field," he admitted.

While he was panicking, Kendra realized. "There must be knives in the kitchen," she said. "We could get one from there."

"Right," agreed Adam. He led the way back. The room was still cheery and neat. "Okay, start looking," he ordered. "We've got to get out of this house."

Kendra and Nicky started to check the drawers under the butcher-block table. Adam was looking under the sink. Nathan and Josh, both trying hard not to shake, headed for what had to be the food pantry.

"The sooner we're out of here the better," Nathan agreed. He jerked open the door, and then Kendra heard both of the boys scream.

She spun around and jumped in shock. Nathan was on the floor, and on top of him was a tattered, ragged, decaying skeleton of a man.

68

CHAPTER 11

"Get it off me!" Nathan screamed, thrashing around. "Get it off me!"

Trying to ignore her own fear and disgust, Kendra went to help him. Nicole simply stood and screamed. Josh whimpered and cowered away from his friend. Only Adam tried to help Kendra. Together—trying not to touch the rotting corpse too much—they managed to get it off Nathan. Nathan immediately scuttled away from it, sniffling and hyperventilating.

"That's got to be the most gross thing I've ever done," Kendra muttered to Adam.

"But you did it," he replied, brushing off his hands and trying not to look at the decaying body. "I'm proud of you."

Kendra didn't know what to say. Instead, she

looked at the corpse from the corner of her eye. "It looks like whoever that was has been dead a very long time."

"Yes," Adam agreed. Kendra was surprised at how he was holding up. "But there's something very odd. There's no stench of decay. Even though the body must be decades old, it doesn't *smell* like it."

Fighting down her disgust, Kendra looked at the corpse. Adam was right, she realized. It *looked* revolting, but it wasn't what she'd expect an ancient corpse to be like. "What do you mean?"

"I don't think that poor soul's been here all this time," Adam said slowly. "I think it was put there for our benefit."

Kendra didn't get his drift. "Why?"

"I don't know that," he told her. "But there's something very odd about this house. Beyond the obvious, I mean. Haven't you noticed that bad things happen to us only when we try to escape? When we simply look around, we find dinner set for us, or beds that are freshly made. It's as if someone or something was trying to make us *want* to stay here. And when we try to get out..."

"Then there're saber-toothed tigers or soldiers waiting for us," Kendra said softly. "And when Nicky tried to burn down the front door, we heard Nathan scream."

"And when we looked for a knife to force the

70

door," Adam added, "we came across a rotting corpse. I think there's something going on here that we haven't figured out yet. Some force trying to keep us in this house for some reason."

Nicky gave another scream, and they stared at her. She glared back at them. "I hate you," she said. "How can you talk like that when so many horrible things are happening to us?"

"Panicking and screaming aren't going to help," Adam pointed out. "We have to think logically if we're ever going to get out of here."

"Not me," Nicky answered. "I've had it. I can't take any more. I'm getting out of this house *now!*" She ran for the back door, and wrenched at the handle.

Kendra felt nothing but pity for her old friend. She'd already tried the door, and it wouldn't open. What chance was there that Nicky could really get out?

To her surprise, the door opened as Nicky tugged at it. Then the girl was through the door and running, not at all caring what lay beyond.

"I don't believe it!" Adam exclaimed. Then he ran for the door, with Kendra right behind him. Josh and Nathan stayed where they were, numb with shock.

There was a jungle outside the back door, and bright sunlight. But it wasn't the same jungle they had seen from the front window. This looked a lot more alien. Instead of trees, there were huge ferns. There were no flowers, but there were odd growths that Kendra couldn't identify. Tall grasses were all over the place, and small pools of mud. It had obviously finished raining quite recently—wherever this was.

As Kendra stared out, she saw something moving in the jungle. She gasped in shock as a huge insect buzzed between the trees. She'd caught a glimpse of something that was a shimmering blue color, and at least a foot from wing to wing. There were no such insects. It looked like a dragonfly, but it was way too big for one. Nothing like that had lived since . . .

Since the days of dinosaurs . . .

"Oh my God," she whispered, going pale. They already knew that this house opened up in different eras. Had they somehow now emerged into the Jurassic age? What else lay out there, besides the dragonfly and the weird plants? And Nicky, running for her life? Kendra looked at Adam. "We've got to go after her," she said firmly. "I think she's in terrible danger."

"It figures," agreed Adam. Turning around, he growled, "Josh, get over here. Now!" Josh stumbled across the kitchen. He avoided looking at the spot where the ancient corpse had fallen. "Keep this door open," Adam ordered. "I don't care how, just do it. And watch for us coming back." He turned back to Kendra, and swallowed.

"Okay," he said reluctantly. "I guess I'm as ready as I'll ever be. Let's go and find her."

Nathan and Josh looked less than happy about being left behind with the body. On the other hand, neither of them wanted to venture out into the jungle. Both seemed to be on the verge of fainting. Kendra didn't have any sympathy left inside her for either of them. As for Nicky—part of her wanted to just shut the door and ignore the idiot. But the better part of her nature knew she'd never do that. Even if whatever happened was Nicky's own fault, she couldn't just let the other girl pay for her stupidity with her life.

By Adam's side, Kendra stepped out of the house and into the jungle. The first thing that struck her was the heat. It had to be ninety degrees out here! She'd dressed warmly, expecting a cool October night when she'd left home. Here and now, it felt like midsummer. She wiped her forehead and wished she'd worn a lighter T-shirt.

Then there were the smells. There was a stench of rotting vegetation all around them. Kendra noticed that there was mud and small pools of water that squelched under her sneakers as she walked along. At least Nicky's footprints were really easy to see. "I think we're on the edge of a swamp here," she muttered.

"It certainly smells like it," agreed Adam. Then he slapped at his neck. "Mosquitos, I guess," he

73

said. "Terrific. The sooner we find Nicole, the better."

There was a cry from just ahead, and then a loud splash. Kendra sighed. "I guess that must be her." She started off at a slow trot. If she went much faster, she'd be exhausted in this heat.

Together they pushed along the small trail and into a tiny clearing. When she saw Nicky, Kendra couldn't help smiling. The other girl had tripped over one of the larger trees' roots and gone sprawling in a pool of stinky mud. She was covered in the smelly, wet goo, and trying to stagger out of the pool. It was just what she deserved for being such a jackass.

"We'd better give her a hand," said Adam reluctantly. "I wish I'd brought nose plugs, though."

Kendra held out a hand to Nicky. "Well," she commented, "you really are a stinker this time. Come on." Nicky's slimy hand fastened on hers and she gave the other girl a tug. As Nicky lurched free of the sticky mud with a *gloop,* Adam helped steady her. Nicky was beyond words now. She stood there, shaking and shivering, too worn down by her miseries to even make a comment.

"Back we go," Adam said gently. "You can probably wash up in the house."

Nicky didn't even protest. She simply trudged along beside Kendra. She squelched with every step, her sneakers obviously filled with the mud.

It wasn't difficult to retrace their steps. A few moments later, they could see what must be the house ahead of them. It wasn't the house they'd entered by; it looked more like a cave now, but still in roughly the same shape as the house. And there was an open door, with a very nervous Nathan standing in it. It looked almost inviting to Kendra. For all the horrors inside, they would at least be safe from the worst horrors out here. And she realized that, somehow, the house probably looked different in each of the time periods it took them to, fitting in with the setting.

And then Kendra heard the soft, throaty roar from behind them. She whirled around, and froze solid in her tracks.

Twenty feet away, watching them carefully with glittering, hungry eyes, stood a dinosaur. Kendra wasn't really sure what species it was, because she'd never been interested in them. On the other hand, there was no mistaking *what* it was—its long, green snout was filled with sharp, pointed teeth; its front feet had razor-sharp claws on them, and its tail was swishing from side to side as it stood ready to pounce.

It was obviously a meat-eater.

And the three of them were meat . . .

CHAPTER 12

"Run!" yelled Adam.

"Run yourself," snapped Kendra. Ignoring the panic that she felt in her stomach, she gave Nicky a hefty push. Then, watching the predator as it hissed and snorted, she snatched up a length of deadwood from the ground. She could hear Nicky splashing her way back toward the house, but she didn't dare take her eyes off the dinosaur.

Its eyes moved to watch her as she hefted the large stick. Carefully, she started to back toward the house. Adam was somewhere behind her, but she didn't dare a look to see just where he was or what he was doing. All of her attention was focused on the creature that was staring intently at her. She couldn't help wishing she hadn't seen *Jurassic Park* on video again the other night.

How far did she have to walk backward? About sixty feet, if she remembered correctly. But how far would this monster let her move before it realized its supper was getting away? It was just as tall as she was, but it certainly looked a lot meaner. With those claws and teeth, if it got close to her she wouldn't stand a chance. And here she was trying to fend it off with a stick . . .

Step by step, she backed toward the house. She didn't dare look away from the dinosaur. For the moment it seemed puzzled by her reaction. Maybe it was used to prey that either ran for their lives or else stood their ground to fight. Or maybe she just smelled wrong to it or something. After all, if this was the age of the dinosaurs, there were no mammals around that were bigger than squirrels. It might not even be certain that it really wanted to eat her.

She hoped.

The creature hissed again, and she saw its purple tongue flicker out of its mouth. Then it took a single step, and she could hear it sniffing the air. Its snout wrinkled as it did so, and she knew for certain it was going to attack.

Kendra didn't have time to panic or scream. She looked quickly over her shoulder and saw that she was now within about thirty feet of the back door. Adam was off to one side of her, and slightly closer to the house. She couldn't see Nicky, Josh, or Nathan. They were probably hiding somewhere, scared out of whatever wits they had left. At least the back door was still open, though. Then she glanced back at the dinosaur, just in time to see it begin its charge.

It ran on its two large back legs, the front legs out, claws clicking, ready to rip into her. It roared, opening its huge mouth and giving her a terrifying view of its teeth. She didn't have a hope of being able to make it back to the house before it caught up with her. Trying to stay as calm as she could, she gripped the branch she held tightly, and prepared to defend herself. Thank goodness she had a pretty good swing in baseball!

The monster was only about five feet from her when a rock slammed into its head, and she heard Adam holler in triumph. The rock was fist-sized, and traveling with plenty of force. It bounced off the dinosaur, but left a long, bleeding gash on the creature's temple. It gave a terrible howl and paused in its tracks, obviously unsettled by this attack from the side.

All of Kendra's anger and fear had built up within her, and she could take no more. She needed to explode and let it all out. Without even thinking, she gave a howl and stepped forward, whipping around the stick she held in a wicked swing.

The end of the branch caught the hunter on the jaw. The wood cracked and shattered under the impact. Kendra felt the shock from the blow

78

all the way up her arms and into her shoulders. She'd put all of her strength and fear and fury into hitting the dinosaur. The shock made her drop the branch, leaving her defenseless.

But it also sent her attacker sprawling. The blow had caught it completely unawares, and it went flying and screaming. Before it could recover, Kendra turned and ran as fast as she could for the back door of the cave. Her lungs burned from the strain, and she was dripping a river of sweat. But if she didn't make it back in time, she was dead meat. Out of the corner of her eye, she saw that Adam was racing along with her. There was another howl of anger and frustration behind them, and she heard the dinosaur clamber to its feet again and start after them.

She could see the open door ahead. Would she be able to make it in time? Any second now she might feel those razorlike claws ripping into her back, or those fangs sinking into her neck! Heart pounding, stomach churning, she raced for the door.

And then she was through it, skidding on the polished kitchen floor. Adam was barely a second behind her, and he paused only to slam the door closed. There was the sound of a click as the lock caught. Then there was a loud crash as the hunter slammed into the door. They had made it to safety just in the nick of time.

Kendra collapsed onto the floor, panting and

sweating like crazy. Her whole body felt weak, and she was trembling. She'd almost been lunch for a dinosaur! If it hadn't been for Adam's well-placed thrown rock, she might be lying dead outside now, her bones being gnawed on by that predator. She owed her life to him.

She found herself looking into his worried eyes. "You okay?" he gasped, between pants for breath.

"Yeah," she managed. "Thanks."

He stroked her cheek gently. "You're crazy," Adam said. But he sounded proud of her.

"So are you," she replied. "And you throw a mean curve ball." Kendra looked around the kitchen. Nathan, Josh, and Nicky were hiding behind the butcher block, shaking. "You were all a great help," she muttered, finally getting to her feet. She was starting to feel halfway normal again. Marching across to them, she glared down at Nicky. "I know you're frightened, but if you do one more stupid thing I will personally feed you to that monster out there. Got that straight?"

Nicky didn't answer. She just whimpered, and tears ran down her cheeks. "I'm scared," she finally managed to say.

"We're *all* scared," Kendra told her. "You think I get a thrill trying to avoid being a dinosaur's lunch? Just try and *think* before you panic next time, will you?" Ignoring the three quivering wrecks, she turned back to Adam. It was amazing how dependent on him she was becoming. But he was smart, brave, and levelheaded—everything the trio she'd always considered her friends weren't. Boy, had she ever made a mistake in choosing who to hang out with! She turned to smile at Adam. Despite having messed up with him, she felt a lot closer to him than to her so-called friends. "Well, we're all back together at least. And I don't think Nicky is going to do anything else stupid. Not if she wants to stay in one piece, anyway. So—do you have any idea what we should try next?"

"Strangely enough, yes," Adam answered. He gestured toward the pantry door. "Am I the only one who's noticed that the body has vanished?"

Kendra stared, and saw that he was right: the wizened corpse was gone. "Did one of you do that?" she asked.

"Are you kidding?" asked Nathan, shuddering at the thought. "No way would we have touched that thing."

Adam smiled. "It's gone because there's no need for it any more," he said. "Whatever is doing all this to us has a plan of some kind in mind. That body only appeared when we were looking for a way out of this house. Now that we're back, it's vanished. I think that there's some force at work here that wants us to stay."

"It's got a funny way of asking us to hang out," muttered Kendra.

"Yes, it does," agreed Adam. "But I don't think it knows any other way. We've been threatened when we try to leave and we've been promised nice things if we stay—like that hot dinner. I think that there's somebody in this house that wants us desperately to stay here. And I think I know where he or she must be hiding."

CHAPTER 13

"So don't keep us in suspense," Kendra said. "Where?"

"When I was running back to the house," Adam said, taking his sweet time about it, "I noticed something strange. There are four windows on the floor upstairs, but only three down here. And then I realized that we'd discovered four rooms upstairs on each side, but only three downstairs."

"So?" asked Nathan, annoyed. "It doesn't mean anything. The rooms don't have to be the same size."

"No," Adam agreed calmly. "But I tried to work it out mentally. I think that there's definitely at least ten more feet upstairs than downstairs."

"That doesn't make sense," Kendra said. "So

what you're trying to say is that you think there's a hidden room down here somewhere?"

"I knew you'd figure it out," Adam said proudly. "Yeah, that's exactly what I think. When I was running toward the house, there was an upstairs window at the south end of the house that didn't have a window underneath it. I think that there's some sort of hidden room behind the kitchen here and behind the library. I think that whoever is behind all the weird things that have been happening in this house is in there. And I think that if we find a way into that room, then we might find the way out of this house."

Kendra looked at the wall in the kitchen that he'd mentioned. It looked perfectly normal to her eyes. "Behind that?" she asked. "What do you want to do—take an ax to it?"

"No," admitted Adam. "It does look pretty solid. But I'll bet it's accessible through the library."

"Why?" demanded Josh.

Adam grinned. "That's where secret passages are always hidden in detective movies," he said.

Nicky scowled at him. "Aren't you going to take this seriously?" she demanded.

"Very serious," he replied. "Come on—let's start hunting."

He led the way across the hall and into the library again. Kendra saw that the Mark Twain book was still there and still open. She couldn't help shivering. It was as if somebody here could read her every thought and secret. How else could they know about the book and the page she'd left off at? She just hoped that Adam's belief that there was someone behind all this was true. If there wasn't a human being involved . . . then she simply didn't know what to think.

"Start hunting for anything on the south wall that might be a hidden door," Adam ordered.

Kendra looked at it. It was filled with bookcases, except for the small gap where the fireplace was. This had the makings of a fire in it, but nothing more. At least there wasn't a blaze going! That would have complicated their search. As the others all moved to start examining the cases, Kendra walked across to the fireplace. She realized that this was probably the least likely place a hidden entrance would be. In this house, then, that made it the *most* likely place, since nothing here seemed to be normal.

It seemed to Kendra that they had been in the house forever. She had changed so much since she'd stupidly walked in through that front door. Adam had been right—in the past, she'd let her so-called friends do her thinking for her. Even when she'd known that they were wrong, she'd gone along with their dumb ideas and moronic jokes. And look where that had landed her! She resolved never to do that again. From now on, she'd make her own decisions. And if other people didn't like what she decided to do—well, that was their problem.

One thing she knew—her friendship with Nicky, Josh, and Nathan was well and truly over. The three of them had turned out to be real pains in the butt...as well as jerks and cowards. Friends like that nobody needed. On the other hand, Adam had shown himself to possess courage, brains, and a surprising amount of humor. She knew she had grown rather fond of him during their time here, which surprised her a lot. Earlier today, she wouldn't have given him a second thought. Now she was glad he was willing to forgive her stupidity and go out with her. It was strange how things like that happened.

She could *almost* like this house for making her wise up.

Kendra explored every inch of the fireplace as she thought about all these things. There was no sign of a hidden catch on the mantel, or above it on the wall. That left the fireplace itself. It was large enough for her to walk into. The makings of the fire were laid out near the front. She carefully skirted those and walked behind them and into the back of the large fireplace. It looked like there was nothing back there but the solid stones that made up the chimney. Still, she couldn't overlook anything. One by one, she pressed both sides of each stone in case one of them was on a hinge of some kind, but she didn't really expect that to be the case.

So when one of the stones actually gave way, she almost fell down.

The stone had pivoted about a hinge in the center, and revealed a small space behind. Excitedly, Kendra peered inside it. "I've got it!" she exclaimed. "There's a switch hidden here."

"All right!" said Adam, enthusiastically. He and the others crossed the room to join her. "Now we're really going to discover the secret of this place."

"Here goes," said Kendra, feeling the excitement mounting inside her. She pressed down on the switch.

With a low, groaning noise, the entire back of the fireplace swung around on its axis, revealing a darkness beyond.

"This is it," Kendra said, leaning forward. "It's back here! I—"

She gave a sudden scream as a skeletally thin hand suddenly emerged from out of the darkness and gripped her wrist in a hold of steel.

CHAPTER 14

Kendra screamed again, and tried to get free of the hand. Despite the fact that it looked barely more than skin over ancient bones, the grip was too strong for her to break. As she pulled, though, the rest of the hand's owner came into view, which made her shriek more.

It was a man, but an incredibly ancient one. He was barely more than a skeleton covered with paper-thin skin. His veins showed through his skin, and Kendra would have thought he was dead except that he had astonishingly piercing blue eyes that locked onto hers. The ancient, wrinkled face almost split as his lips moved. In a thin, whispery voice, he said, "Please! I mean you no harm! Believe me!"

The first shock of being touched by this almost

dead man was wearing off, and Kendra was able to force her panic down and stop screaming. Adam was with her then, his face twisted in concern for her. She managed to gasp, "It's okay. I was just . . . startled." She stared at the wizened, ancient features of the man who had emerged from the darkness. "I don't think he could hurt me if he wanted to."

The old face split and a wheezing sound came out of it. Kendra realized the old man was laughing. "It's true," he gasped. "My strength is almost gone. I don't have a lot of time left to me. Twenty years at most."

"Twenty years?" echoed Adam. "That sounds like a lot of time to me."

The old man gave his wheezing laugh again as he released his grip on Kendra's hand. He was sitting against one wall of the fireplace, obviously not strong enough to get to his feet unaided. "But that is because you are young," the man answered. "Unlike me. I am older than you could imagine."

"Trust me," Kendra told him, "after the time we've spent in this house, there's very little that would surprise me now."

The man nodded. "I imagine you are correct," he agreed. "Know then that I am Jeremiah Clarke. I was born in the year of our Lord 1754."

"Jeez," whispered Adam. "You mean you're over two hundred years old?"

"Yes." The old man nodded. "I am indeed. And I've been trapped in this house almost all of that time."

Kendra felt a chill pass through her. "Jeremiah Clarke?" she said. "The same one whose name is in the family bible out there in the library?"

"The same," he confirmed. "My family owned this house for two centuries. Or *it* owned them."

"Then can you explain what's going on in this place?" asked Adam. "We've had some really crazy things happen since we came in the front door."

"Explain?" Old Jeremiah nodded. Then he looked tired. "That I can. But, if you would be so kind, my weary old bones would rather be resting in a chair than on these cold stones."

"Oh, sure." Kendra felt guilty that she hadn't thought of that. "Why were you in here anyway?" She and Adam helped Jeremiah to his unsteady feet.

"The house tricked me to get me in here," he explained as he shuffled across to the nearest chair with their help. "It didn't want me to warn you of what was going to happen before it trapped you."

Kendra shivered again. "You . . . you make it sound as if the house is alive."

"Aye," agreed Jeremiah. "And for good reason—this accursed house *is* alive." Kendra and Adam gasped, and she heard Nicky, Nathan, and

90

Josh gasp behind them. So they were listening to all of this too. They hadn't come to her help, she realized. Only Adam had possessed enough courage for that.

Jeremiah managed another of his wheezing laughs. "Well, maybe not alive as you and I are. Or even like an animal is. But this house is alive, nonetheless. It's a strange creature, not really rational. But it has a spirit, and powers that few people could even guess at. And, worse than anything else, it has a terrible hunger."

"It wants to *eat* us?" shrieked Nicky.

"Not that kind of hunger, lass," Jeremiah told her. "Worse. If it wanted only to consume you, then your suffering would be done in minutes. No, the hunger that this house holds is for people to be in it. And that can last almost forever. Like I told you, I'm more than two hundred years old. The house has kept me alive for that long."

"Then I was right," Adam said. "The intelligence here wants us to stay. It doesn't want to hurt us."

"Hurt you?" Jeremiah rattled off his dusty laugh again. "Nay—that it doesn't. You'd be of no use to it if you were injured or dead. It needs you as you are—well and intact. And it will make you stay here for the rest of your lives. And in this house that will be longer—a lot longer—than you think. Two, maybe three hundred years. Some have lasted longer, I've been told."

91

Kendra swallowed hard, trying to avoid panicking. Old Jeremiah sounded so certain, but some of the things he was claiming weren't exactly sensible. "Who told you?" she asked. "How do you know all of this?"

The old man smiled. "You think I'm crazy, don't you?" he asked gently. "Well, I'm not surprised. Or upset, either. When I was first told this, I thought the person who informed me was as mad as a hatter, too." He cackled. "But I'm not demented, believe you me."

"We would, if you made some sense," Adam said gently. "Why don't you start at the beginning, then, and tell us what you're talking about."

"Aye," Jeremiah agreed. "I am rambling a bit. Well, little wonder, since I've had no other human to speak to in almost fifty years." He sighed. "This house has always been here," he explained. "It didn't always look the way it does now, but it's astonishingly ancient. It has a mind of sorts, and an intelligence. It is neither good nor evil. It just *is*. You can talk to it, in a way, if you try hard enough. Its mind doesn't work like ours, but it can think and plan. And it's terribly hungry for company. That's why it keeps people here.

"I know it's truthful, because it doesn't seem to even understand the idea of lying, but some of the things it's told me have gone against everything I've ever been taught from science or the Bible. It claims to be millions and millions of

92

years old. That life once began on this planet that long and longer ago. I've seen some of the creatures that the house knew if I look from the windows. Some of them look like giant lizards, and others like lions with huge fangs. There are so many strange animals that can be seen that I'm inclined to believe the house. Such creatures never lived while men were on this earth.

"This house was a very ancient form of life even then. It can't remember ever being born, and it never grows old or feeble. But it's lonely, because it is the only one of its kind in this world of ours. Before people came along, it thought that it would always be alone. It would howl out its despair in the dark of night. Then, when it discovered people, it found that it could interact with them. It disguised itself as a type of dwelling place for the native people of this land, and lured them within. The Indians who lived in these parts realized that it was cursed, and stayed away. When the Europeans came to this country, they refused to listen to the warnings that the wiser natives gave them, and some stumbled into the house. There they stayed, their lives lengthened by the house. But the house can only manipulate time. It can't defeat it. They grew old, and died, and the house was alone again.

"Then I stumbled into it." He sighed, a deep, brooding sound, filled with pain and regret. "It was in 1778, and I was fleeing the redcoats. I needed somewhere to hide, and I didn't know the stories about this house. I ran inside, and then discovered that I was unable to leave. The house had a captive soul again, and it would never set me free while I lived.

"In its own way, I suppose the house is good to me. There is always fine food to eat, and books to read. My bed was made every night. But it would never allow me to leave, because it knew that if I did, I would never return and it would be alone again." He gave another wheezing laugh. "But I will win in the end," he said, giving a toothy grin. "I cannot live much longer, no matter how much this house plays with time. I shall die soon—in the next twenty years or so—and then I shall be free again."

Jeremiah looked up at them sharply. "You've seen how it plays tricks with time?" he asked.

"Yes," Kendra replied. "From each window and door, it seems to open onto a different era in time. All but the one we come from."

"That lies through the front door alone," Jeremiah informed them. "But it will never allow you to return through it."

"Why not?" yelped Nicky. "I want to go home!"

Jeremiah snorted. "Home?" He shook his head, making his wispy white hair shimmer. "Lass, you'd better get used to this house. It's going to be your home from now until you die."

94

He stared back at their horrified expressions. "It means to keep you here forever," he told them. "So that when I die it will not be alone. All five of you are trapped here in this dreadful house until you eventually age, wither, and die. It may take two hundred years, if you're lucky. But you all look strong. I'd bet you'll last here four hundred or more ... slowly going madder and more desperate every single day of every single year...."

CHAPTER
15

Kendra was almost overcome by the thought of being trapped here for centuries, unable to leave. All of the horror and scares they had experienced so far seemed to weigh down on her courage, shrinking it so that all she wanted to do was scream and run around in a mad panic. What snapped her out of this was hearing Nicky howl in terror and despair. Kendra managed to fight down her own terrors, determined that she would not sink to the same level as Nicky.

Adam was looking pale and shaken, too, but he managed to give her a small smile of encouragement. "You're absolutely sure that this is what the house aims to do?" he asked Jeremiah. "You're not just trying to scare us?"

"No, lad," he replied, shaking his head. "The

house is very clear about that. It thinks that with you five, it'll never have to be alone again."

The idea was so horrifying that Kendra didn't know what to say. To be kept here, in this nightmarish house, like an animal in a cage. And for century after century! She knew she'd go mad. She was amazed that Jeremiah was still so rational, after 200 years.

"It's not going to happen," said Adam flatly. "How do you manage to talk to the house?" he asked the old man. "It doesn't seem to want to speak to us."

"It takes a bit of getting used to," Jeremiah admitted. "It talks in your mind, kind of like an itchy feeling in the back of your head. Then words and ideas form." He gestured with a shaking hand to the hidden room behind the fireplace. "Back there's where I hear it most," he explained. "It's quiet and dark and private in there. Less distractions, I suppose."

Nodding, Adam crossed to the fireplace. "I'm going to try and talk to it," he told Kendra. "Maybe it will let us go if I ask nicely. You just keep an eye on the others. Make sure they don't do anything stupid, okay?"

"Okay," she agreed, eyeing Nicky, Josh, and Nathan. Nicky had settled down to a quiet sobbing now.

Adam nodded and vanished into the hole behind the fireplace. Kendra swallowed, and alter-

97

nated between watching her charges and looking for his return. Jeremiah seemed to have slumped almost into sleep, huddled in the chair. It seemed to last forever, but it could only have been about ten minutes before Adam, shaking, stumbled out. With a cry of concern, Kendra ran across to help him. He needed support to cross to the closest available chair, and his skin felt cold and goose bumpy.

"I'll be okay," he managed to gasp. "It was just so . . . strange." Then he smiled slightly. "But I did it—I talked to the house."

"Will it let us go?" asked Kendra anxiously.

Adam shook his head, defeating all her hopes. "No. Jeremiah is right; it's going to keep us here forever." He sighed. "This house is like a shell around the creature within. Like a hermit crab. Hermit!" He laughed sharply. "I felt this terrible, hollow loneliness inside of it, Kendra. Like it has no friends and doesn't hope to ever have any." He shuddered. "That's something I know about. I've never had many friends, but I've never been that terribly lonely."

Kendra grabbed his ice-cold hand. "You've got at least one friend now," she told him. "I promise."

"Thanks," he replied, managing a real smile this time. "And I'm more glad of that than you can imagine." Reluctantly, he let go of her hand. "But we've got work to do."

"What work?" asked Nathan. "You just said that this stinking house won't ever let us go."

"I said it won't *let* us go," Adam agreed. "But I have absolutely no intention of staying here forever." He grinned at Kendra. "I want to take you to a movie tomorrow night, and there's no theater in here. Heck, there's not even a TV."

Jeremiah roused himself. "Haven't you been paying attention?" he asked. "If you try and escape, the house will stop you. If it can't have you, it's quite willing to kill you."

"I'll take that chance," Adam answered. He glanced at Kendra, and she nodded. She'd run any risk to avoid staying here for the rest of her life. "How about the rest of you?" he asked.

Nathan and Josh stared at one another. They were still in shock, but they both managed to nod. Nicky simply sat on the floor, tears trickling down her face.

"Let's take it as a yes," Kendra sighed. Poor Nicky was too far gone to object.

Jeremiah shook his head. "You're young and you're headstrong," he said. "So I suppose you have to try. I tried to escape when I first came here. Now I know escape is impossible."

Adam got to his feet and crossed to his chair. Patting Jeremiah kindly on the hand, he said, "With all due respect, sir, I think that we may have a few ideas you've never thought of in the past." He grinned. "I think Kendra and I together

99

could solve any problem." Kendra blushed at this praise. He really did have a high opinion of her.

The old man sighed again. "Well, I can't stop you," he said. "I wish you luck, though. To escape . . ." He shook his head and slowly clambered to his feet. "I don't mean to sound like a pessimist, but the house is going to try and kill you to stop you. I'd feel a lot safer in my little hideaway." Adam helped him back to the fireplace. Jeremiah shook his head. "I'll be seeing you again soon," he said. "Dead or alive. Alive, I hope, but dead I fear." Then he passed into the darkness beyond. With a grating sound, the fireplace slid back to cover the hidden room.

"Cheery soul, isn't he?" asked Adam. "Well, luckily I have more faith in our abilities. Let's try the kitchen again for a knife. Even if we can't pry the lock off the front door, we could use it as a screwdriver and take the lock apart."

Kendra nodded, and fell in beside him as he marched back across the hallway. She saw out of the corner of her eye that the other three were reluctantly dragging their feet along behind them. Kendra knew that the house would try and stop them. It always had. But how far would it go? Would it really try to kill them?

As they opened the door to the kitchen, Kendra gasped.

The back door of the house was open, and beyond it lay the dinosaur swamps.

In the doorway stood the angry, hungry hunter they had barely escaped from before. It still had a bleeding gash above the eye where Adam's rock had hit it. With a roar, it took a step into the kitchen.

The house was letting it in—so that it could hunt them!

Adam pushed Kendra back roughly, and then slammed the kitchen door shut. Gripping the handle, he gasped, "We've got to get away from it! Think!"

Kendra didn't know *what* to think. The predatory dinosaur was after them! She heard it slam its way across the kitchen to the door.

Adam gasped as the handle started to turn under his hand. "The door!" he exclaimed. "It's opening by itself! The house *wants* that monster to get us!"

CHAPTER 16

Kendra thought fast. Whirling around, she ordered Josh, Nicky, and Nathan, "Upstairs! Find somewhere to hide! Maybe that monster will be confused when it's faced with steps!" Then she tried to help Adam hold the door closed. But she could feel that it was no use. The house was much stronger than they were, and the door was starting to inch open. She heard three sets of footsteps hurtling up the stairs, then gave Adam an agonized look. "I think we'd better go now."

"Right," he agreed. They both released the door, which whipped open. It caught the lurking dinosaur full in the jaw, sending it sprawling across the kitchen. It screamed out at them.

"Hasn't improved its mood any," Kendra muttered as she turned and raced for the stairs. Adam was beside her all the way. There was no sign of the others when they reached the top, but they could hear the dinosaur slamming its way across the kitchen and onto their trail again.

"This way," Adam suggested, pointing to the room on the right. He dived inside. Kendra followed and was about to close the door and look for something to barricade themselves in with when he stopped her. "No," he said. "Leave it open."

"Then that thing will come in!" Kendra objected.

"I want it to," Adam answered. "Look, we can't hide from it forever, can we? The house will open any doors, and I'm sure it can guide the monster to us if it really wants to. We have to get rid of it somehow." He crossed to the window and opened it. Then he pointed to the rope of sheets she'd made earlier. "Tie one end of that to the bed's leg," he instructed. "Then hide under the bed. The dinosaur should come after me."

Kendra didn't know what he intended to do, but it had to be dangerous. On the other hand, what choice did they have? And there was no time to argue. Grabbing her end of the sheets, she started to tie the strongest knot around the leg closest to the window. She strained her ears to hear what the dinosaur was doing, but she didn't have to concentrate that hard. It was roaring and hissing away, and she heard its thumping steps on the stairs. "It's coming!" she gasped as she slipped under the bed.

"Okay." Adam took a deep breath. "Wish me luck," he muttered, "because I'm sure going to need it." He walked slowly back to the door, and then out at the stairs. From where she lay under the bed, she could see from the expression on his face that the hunter was in sight. "Here I am, you dumb reptile!" he yelled, waving his hands. "Come and get me! Lunch time!" Then: "Uh-oh!" as he dived back into the room and across to the window. Gripping the end of the sheet rope, he sprang into the large open window frame, and stared back across the room.

With a furious roar, the predator crashed its way into the room. Its jaw was working, and its tongue was flickering like a snake's as it sensed food. The beast's eyes narrowed as it stared at its prey in the window, and then it threw itself across the room in a terrifying leap.

Kendra almost fainted from the shock. At the last second, Adam dived out of the window, clutching onto the sheet for dear life. The dinosaur had missed its target, but it managed to stop itself from going out the window after him. Teetering on the sill, it swayed there, hissing and howling.

Adam's plan wasn't working! He had hoped that the monster would fall out of the window and be unable to get back inside. But it was still there!

She had no choice. Kendra wriggled out from under the bed, and with a yell of rage and fear, she charged at the window. The dinosaur heard her coming from behind and tried to twist around to attack her. That made it wobble even more. Kendra slammed into its back with her shoulder, pushing as hard as she could. The predator toppled, finally, squealing loudly as it lost its balance and fell. The creature's thrashing tail gave her a stinging blow to her shoulder, and sent her sprawling across the floor and onto the bed. She heard the monster hit the ground like a runaway train, and there was silence for a moment.

Fighting down the pain in her shoulder, Kendra forced herself to get up and hurry back to the window to check on Adam. She stared down, and saw that he was already climbing back up his rope ladder. Beyond him, the dinosaur lay stunned in the yard. But as she watched, it started to shake its head and attempted to stagger to its feet. Adam looked back, and then continued climbing even faster. That monster seemed to be almost unstoppable.

But only almost. Kendra had forgotten about the two redcoat soldiers who had chased Adam and Nathan earlier. They must have been hunting about the house for a way in or some sign of their quarry, because they both came running around the side of the house, obviously drawn by the noise.

They stopped dead in their tracks when they saw the dinosaur getting groggily to its feet. Then, without seeming to think about it, they both whipped their muskets into position and fired at it.

The two bullets crashed into the monster, making it stagger again, roaring in pain and fear. Kendra saw that there were two great gashes in its chest. It still wasn't stopped, however. Realizing it was in danger from the soldiers, the creature started after them. This gave Adam the time he needed to get through the window. Kendra dragged the sheet back inside, but hesitated on closing the window, wanting to witness the end of this hunt.

The two soldiers hastily reloaded their muskets as the dinosaur advanced toward them. Then, one after the other, they fired. The first shot caught the beast in the throat, sending it sprawling. The second shot exploded into the creature's right eye. It must have hit the monster's brain, because it gave one last, feeble howl, and then lay still.

Adam slammed down the window before the soldiers could turn their fire at it. Then he collapsed to the floor, shaking. "That was way too close for me," he gasped. "I feel like I'm made of jelly."

"You're the bravest person I've ever met," Kendra said simply. "I'm very proud of you."

He managed a grin at that. "Flatterer. If you

hadn't tackled that thing from behind, my plan wouldn't have worked, would it?"

"Maybe not," she admitted, wincing at the pain in her shoulder. "On the other hand, at least you *had* a plan."

"Well, I guess that means we're a terrific team, doesn't it!" Adam scrambled to his feet. "Now, how about this terrific team putting both its brains together and coming up with an escape plan. I'm not so sure I want to risk going into the kitchen again after a knife."

"I know what you mean," Kendra agreed. "If the house knows what we're going to do, it can try and stop us." Then she snapped her fingers. "That's it!" she exclaimed. "Everytime we've planned something, we always explain it to each other. The house must be able to hear us somehow, and then it can stop us." She gave Adam a smile as inspiration struck her. "Okay. I've got a plan now, but I'm not going to explain it. Let's find the others and get out of here."

"I'm all for that." Adam was obviously dying of curiosity, but he agreed with her opinion and didn't ask for any explanations. As they left the bedroom, he called out for Nicky, Josh, and Nathan. A moment later, the three of them warily emerged from the end room on the left.

"You're safe for now," Kendra told them. "The dinosaur's dead. Now, we're going to march down the stairs and to the front door. I don't want any

questions, because I'm not going to explain anything at all. Let's go." Then she ignored them
completely, and started down the stairs. They either followed or didn't, and she didn't care much
which they chose. Adam was beside her, and he
was the only one she cared about.

What would the house do now? If it didn't
know what her plan was, it wouldn't be able to
stop her directly.

Of course, there were still plenty of other things
it might be able to do. . . .

As she reached the bottom of the stairs, Kendra
hesitated. She glanced toward the front door. The
pile of junk from Nathan's backpack was still
there, as was the hurricane lamp that Nicky had
intended to throw at the door. Perfect.

There was a sudden loud screaming, like all the
ghosts of the dead had been let loose in the
house. Kendra couldn't help jumping at the horrifying noise.

The door beside her suddenly opened, and a
moldering corpse fell out of it and right on top
of her.

108

CHAPTER 17

With a scream that was more rage than fear, Kendra pushed the rotting body aside. "You can't scare me any more!" she yelled at the house. "We're going to beat you, no matter how many tricks you play! We're getting out of here." She ran the rest of the way to the pile of joke stuff that Nathan had brought. She snatched up one of the two spray cans of luminous paint, and placed it against the front door. The second she handed to Adam. "For safe keeping," she said.

Adam nodded. From the look in his eyes, she could see that he'd worked out what she was going to do. She'd realized that although Nicky's idea of trying to burn down the front door was much too dangerous, there was another way of trying it. The paint in the spray can was under pressure. Kendra knew that there were warning labels telling people not to leave the can near flames in case it exploded.

But she *wanted* it to explode. The force of the blast would hopefully wreck at least the lock on the front door. Then they'd be able to break it down and get out.

"Everyone into the library and take cover," she ordered. "And don't move until you hear the door blown open." Josh, Nicky, and Nathan didn't need any more urging. They all vanished into the room, looking rather green. Adam stood beside her.

"Smart girl," he said approvingly. "I think it'll work."

"It had better," Kendra answered. She had no more ideas left in her. But as she started to cross to the table where the lamp was still burning, she heard a sound from the sitting room.

The window opening . . .

"Jeez!" she yelped. The house might not know what she had planned, but it was aiming to stop her any way it could. Maybe it was really scared of a fire. If the house caught fire, would it kill whatever creature lived inside it? As she grabbed the lamp, the door to the room opened.

Inside it stood the saber-toothed tiger, its fangs glistening and its body ready to spring.

There was no way that she'd be able to make it back to safety in time.

110

The tiger was crouched, ready to pounce. Kendra knew she was dead meat. Then she heard Adam howl and shake the paint can. Before the tiger could pounce, Adam sprayed the luminous paint right into its face.

The sabertooth screamed in pain and confusion as the paint hit it in the eyes. It batted at the spray with one huge paw, but yowled when it couldn't stop the attack. Kendra dived to one side, as the blinded beast struck out at them both with its long, razor-sharp claws. One blow barely missed her. The cat moved into the corridor, blocking her escape to the library. It was having trouble with its eyes, but it could obviously still sense her somehow. Probably through scent.

Adam grabbed Kendra and dragged her back toward the front door, still spraying at the tiger with the can he held. "Come on, you stupid beast!" he yelled. "If you want to stop me, you're going to have to fight!" Kendra couldn't imagine what he was trying to do—provoke the monster into attacking them?

And then she understood. Hefting the burning lamp she still held, she threw it at the floor right behind the cat. It shattered, spraying glass everywhere, and then the oil gushed out, catching fire instantly.

There was a wall of flames behind the sabertooth. Like most animals, it was terrified of fire and only wanted to get away.

111

It threw itself at its tormentors.

"Down!" yelled Adam, but Kendra was already in motion. She threw herself forward, under the leaping tiger, and stayed down. She didn't dare run, because flames were all over the rest of the corridor.

The tiger missed them both completely. It was blinded by panic and the paint. Instead, it slammed with all of its might into the front door. The monster had to weigh over six hundred pounds. The door, strong as it was, wasn't any match for the impact of the sabertooth.

In a splintering wrench, the whole door crashed down, flinging the startled cat through the now open gap. Kendra rolled over and jumped to her feet, ready to try and dodge if the tiger attacked again.

But the beast had had enough, it seemed. Instead of turning to attack, the animal fled through the overgrown garden outside.

The overgrown, nighttime, twentieth century garden!

"We're free!" Kendra gasped, rushing for the shattered door. She had to see where the tiger was going. It could attack some innocent passerby ... As she reached for the broken doorway, she was in time to see the tiger leap the low fence and land in the pool of lamplight out in the street. It paused for a second to try and understand what was happening, still pawing at its paint-filled eyes.

And then it was over. One of the huge delivery trucks for the local supermarket was passing. Its headlights lit up the startled tiger, and Kendra heard the scream of brakes. But there was no way that the truck could stop in time. It slammed heavily into the startled tiger. The broken body of the creature flew through the air and into a neighboring garden. The truck, its radiator shattered, gradually slowed to a stop.

Kendra let out her breath in a whoop. "Poor thing," she gasped. But at least it couldn't hurt anyone now.

And they were free.

Josh, Nathan, and Nicky had run from the library when they'd heard the door shatter, obviously thinking that Kendra's plan had worked. Only Josh paused. "Uh . . . thanks," he stammered. "I owe you both." Then he turned and fled past them with the others, down the pathway to freedom without looking back to even check that she and Adam were okay. Well, she wasn't really surprised by Nathan and Nicole's behavior. Only Josh seemed to realize that he owed his life and freedom to them. Standing on the outside of the door to the Hawkins House, Kendra felt all of her fears and tensions evaporating. She reached out her hand to Adam, who still stood inside the house.

"I'm not coming yet," he said gently.

113

"What are you talking about?" she asked, worried. "We've won our freedom."

"Yes, we have," agreed Adam. "And the house knows it. So now I think I'm in a good position to bargain."

"Bargain?" Kendra echoed. "What do you mean?"

His eyes were almost sparkling now. "Time travel," he said. "This house has the ability to make time change. I've *always* loved history, Kendra. And with this house, I could *visit* the times instead of reading about them. Isn't that an incredible thought?"

"Yes," she agreed, feeling some of the wonder he mentioned. "But . . . this house is insane."

"No," he replied. "It's not. It's just horribly lonely. Wait here." He turned to go.

Kendra stepped back into the house. "No way," she replied. "We're a team, remember? I think you're crazy, but I won't let you go back alone."

"You're something special, you know that?" He gave her a reassuring smile, then led the way back to the library. The fire in the hallway had died out, leaving only brown smudges up the walls and across the roof. They seemed to be getting smaller as Kendra watched.

The house was repairing the damage it had suffered, like her body healed scratches. How long would it be before it managed to grow a new front door? Would they have time to escape first?

114

In the library, Adam went to the fireplace and triggered the switch to open the hidden room. Together, they went inside.

It was dark in there, but there was enough light from outside for Kendra to see that there was a chair and table inside it. Jeremiah was sitting in the chair. He shook his head.

"I told you you'd never escape," he said.

"We *did* escape," Kendra informed him. "But we came back."

"Back?" Jeremiah looked startled. "Whatever for?"

"I was kind of wondering that myself," admitted Kendra. She looked hard at Adam.

"House," he said, in a firm, even voice. "We just proved to you that we can escape from here any time we want to. Even if you trap us again, we can still break free. Now, will you listen to what I have to say, or should we just turn around and walk out of here?"

Kendra strained to hear an answer. To her shock, she did. It was like a sighing voice in the back of her mind.

What do you wish to say?

It was the house speaking, and she could hear it!

"We know that you're lonely," Adam said gently. "And I can understand loneliness. I've been pretty lonely in the past, too." He gave Kendra's hand a squeeze. "But I've found a really good

115

friend now. And that's what you need. A *friend.* Not a captive, forced to be here and kept alive artificially. A friend. And that's what I promise I will be. On two conditions."

What conditions? asked the house suspiciously.

"First of all," Adam insisted, "that you stop trying to *keep* me here by force. I have to be free to come and go as I wish. I have a life outside these walls that I don't want to give up. And second, you have to let me explore some of these other time periods when I visit."

And if I agree?

"Then I promise I'll come by often to visit with you and talk to you," Adam answered. "You have a friend and not a captive. And I'll be here because I want to be, not because I'm forced to be."

"Two friends," said Kendra suddenly. She gave Adam a grin. "I'm not going to let you have all the fun on your own."

"Two friends, then," said Adam. "Of our own free will. What do you say?"

There was a long pause, and then another whisper. *I agree,* said the house. *And . . . thank you, friends.* After a pause, the house added: *I think that I have learned something this day, too.*

EPILOGUE: THE MIDNIGHT SOCIETY

And that's about it. Kendra had discovered the true meaning of friendship. And so, strangely enough, had the house. It's amazing, but from that time on, Adam and Kendra had nothing but nice experiences in there. After all, they could have great dinners there, and talk to old Jeremiah Clarke.

The house offered to let him go, too, but he decided that he'd rather stay. He didn't think that the twentieth century was any place for a 200-year-old man. And he now had friends who would visit him.

As for Adam, he'd proven that what terrifies one person might make another one very happy. Kind of like roller-coaster rides, or Halloween scares.

Or tales from the Midnight Society.

That's it for this session, though. It's time to go

home again...to a safe home, not like the Hawkins House as it used to be. And if you happen to pass any old houses on the way home... maybe you'd better stay out of them. Not all of them are just old and abandoned. Some contain horrors like the Hawkins House.

And some, of course, are much, much worse... But if you want to hear about them, then you'll have to come back again for another story from the Midnight Society.

ABOUT THE AUTHOR

John Peel was born in Nottingham, England, home of Robin Hood. He moved to the United States in 1981 to get married and now lives on Long Island with his wife, Nan, and their wirehaired fox terrier, Dashiell. He has written more than fifty books, including novels based on the top British science fiction TV series, *Doctor Who,* and the top American science fiction TV series, *Star Trek.* His novel, *Star Trek: The Next Generation: Here There Be Dragons,* is available from Pocket Books. He has also written several supernatural thrillers for young adults that are published by Archway Paperbacks—*Talons, Shattered, Poison,* and the forthcoming *Maniac.* He has written two stories in the *Star Trek: Deep Space Nine* series for young readers—*Prisoners of Peace* and *Field Trip.*

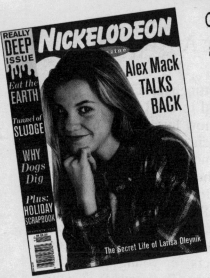

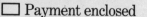

R·L·STINE'S
GHOSTS OF FEAR STREET®

1 HIDE AND SHRIEK 52941-2/$3.99

2 WHO'S BEEN SLEEPING IN MY GRAVE? 52942-0/$3.99

3 THE ATTACK OF THE AQUA APES 52943-9/$3.99

4 NIGHTMARE IN 3-D 52944-7/$3.99

5 STAY AWAY FROM THE TREEHOUSE 52945-5/$3.99

6 EYE OF THE FORTUNETELLER 52946-3/$3.99

7 FRIGHT KNIGHT 52947-1/$3.99

8 THE OOZE 52948-X/$3.99

9 REVENGE OF THE SHADOW PEOPLE 52949-8/$3.99

10 THE BUGMAN LIVES 52950-1/$3.99

11 THE BOY WHO ATE FEAR STREET 00183-3/$3.99

 Available from Minstrel® Books
Published by Pocket Books

POCKET
B O O K S

Simon & Schuster Mail Order Dept. BWB
200 Old Tappan Rd., Old Tappan, N.J. 07675

Please send me the books I have checked above. I am enclosing $_____(please add $0.75 to cover the postage and handling for each order. Please add appropriate sales tax). Send check or money order--no cash or C.O.D.'s please. Allow up to six weeks for delivery. For purchase over $10.00 you may use VISA: card number, expiration date and customer signature must be included.

Name _____

Address _____

City _____ State/Zip _____

VISA Card # _____ Exp.Date _____

Signature _____ 1146-09